GRANDPA'S STOLEN TREASURE

Adventures
of the Northwoods

GRANDPA'S STOLEN TREASURE

Lois Walfrid Johnson

BETHANY HOUSE PUBLISHERS
MINNEAPOLIS, MINNESOTA 55438

Captain Alexander McDougall, a Scottish immigrant, designed and built over forty whalebacks at his American Steel Barge shipyards in Superior, Wisconsin. Assistant Lighthouse Keeper Thomas White was on duty at the Duluth Entry lighthouse during the Mataafa Blow. Captain James Prior was the main keeper during that time. All other characters in this book are fictitious. Any resemblance to persons living or dead is coincidental.

Cover illustration by Andrea Jorgenson.

Published by Bethany House Publishers
A Ministry of Bethany Fellowship, Inc.
6820 Auto Club Road, Minneapolis, Minnesota 55438

Printed in the United States of America

Library of Congress Cataloging-in-Publication Data

Johnson, Lois Walfrid.
    Grandpa's stolen treasure / Lois Walfrid Johnson.
       p.   cm. — (Adventures of the northwoods ; #7)
    Summary: Kate and Anders try to follow the guidance of God when her grandparents travel from Sweden to Wisconsin and Grandma vanishes under mysterious circumstances.
    [1. Swedish Americans—Fiction.] 2. Mystery and detective stories. 3. Christian life—Fiction. 4. Wisconsin—Fiction.] I. Title. II. Series: Johnson, Lois Walfrid. Adventures of the northwoods ; 7.
PZ7.J63255Gr   1992
[Fic]—dc20   92–30093
                                                  CIP
ISBN 1–55661–239–7   AC

To Charette

with many thanks
for your gifts of encouragement

LOIS WALFRID JOHNSON is the author of twenty books, including *You're Worth More Than You Think* and other books in the Let's-Talk-About-It Stories for Kids Series to help preteens make wise choices. Novels in the Adventures of the Northwoods Series have received awards from Excellence in Media, the Wisconsin State Historical Society, and the Council for Wisconsin Writers.

Lois and her husband, Roy, who plays a supportive role in her writing, are the parents of three married children and live in rural Wisconsin.

Contents

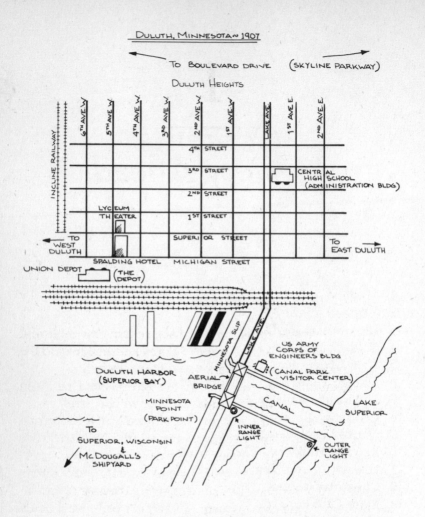

DULUTH, MINNESOTA ~ 1907

If you visit the Twin Ports of Duluth, Minnesota, and Superior, Wisconsin, you'll find that some of the places described in this book have new names. The map on this page will help you follow Kate, Anders, and Erik around the area. The name used during their visit is given first, then the present name.

Whether you've lived in the Twin Ports all your life or are discovering these places for the first time, you, too, can join the search for Grandpa's stolen treasure!

1

Mystery Ahead

*F*rom off in the distance came the mournful cry of a train whistle. As Katherine O'Connell turned toward the sound, her deep blue eyes sparkled with excitement.

"Ten minutes!" she exclaimed to her little sister Tina. "Ten more minutes, and Grandpa and Grandma will be here!"

As though she could speed up the train's arrival, Kate hurried to the edge of the platform. Leaning forward, she tried to see around a building. The Antlers Hotel blocked her view.

In that last week of May 1907, Mama's parents were coming all the way from Sweden. Ever since knowing the time of arrival, Kate had waited for this moment. "If all goes well, we'll be on the midday train," their letter said.

If all goes well, Kate thought now, as she had many times before. *All the way across the Atlantic Ocean. Halfway across America. Would Grandpa and Grandma get here safely?*

As the far-off whistle faded away, Kate walked back to her mother. Mama stood with baby Bernie in her arms. Kate's stepbrothers, thirteen-year-old Anders and nine-year-old Lars, waited nearby, each with his hair combed neatly in place.

Off to one side, Kate's uncle, six feet three inches tall, paced up and down the platform. *It's different for Ben*, Kate thought as she saw his troubled eyes. Kate looked forward to meeting her grandparents. Yet those grandparents were Ben's father and mother. The nineteen-year-old hadn't seen or written to them since running away from home.

Again the train whistle sounded, closer to Grantsburg this time. Above its cry came a high whinny.

Kate's stepfather moved uneasily. "Charlie Saunders got in a railroad car of horses yesterday."

Papa Nordstrom glanced west toward where the livery stable hid beyond the hotel. "Broncos are skittery. Out in Montana they run free till cowboys round them up for branding."

"And Charlie sells them?" Kate asked, curious as always.

Papa nodded. "Sometimes he trains them for people to ride. Other times he sells them right away. When a farmer gets the bronco he wants, he might just take it home and hitch it up with horses that are already trained."

As Kate watched, three men on horseback came into sight on the street leading past the hotel. With four horses trotting between them, the riders turned onto the road on the other side of the tracks. Soon they disappeared behind two potato warehouses.

"They're taking the back way out of town," Papa said. "If they live a few miles out of Grantsburg, they'll drive the horses home."

Just then Tina tugged on Kate's hand. Kate looked down at the five-year-old. "You're tired of waiting, aren't you? Let's race to the street. By the time we get back, the train will be here."

Tina raced off, her white-blond braids bobbing on her shoulders. Kate started after her, then remembered a thirteen-year-old was supposed to act grown up.

Tina kept running. At the end of the platform she jumped into the street. "I won!" she called back. "I got here first!"

Kate grinned and waved. Tina had won, all right.

Before Kate could catch up, a long sharp train whistle pierced the air. Above its call a horse screamed.

Kate glanced around. In the street on this side of the warehouse a large bronco reared up, a wild horse frightened by the train!

Suddenly Kate realized the danger. "Tina!" she called. "Come back!"

A second whistle drowned out her words. Again the horse reared up, pawing the air. Eyes wide, its nostrils flared in fear. As it dropped back to the ground, the bronco bolted.

"Runaway!" a man shouted as he tried to head the bronco off. But the black horse broke through.

"Tina!" Kate cried again as she raced toward her sister. Across the platform and sidewalk Kate flew.

Reaching Tina, Kate grabbed the little girl's arm and pulled her from the street. Seconds later the runaway thundered past.

As Kate dragged Tina onto the platform, she started to whimper. Kneeling down, Kate flung her arms around her. Tina's body shook with sobs.

Kate's arms tightened. "It's all right, Tina. It's all right! You're safe!"

Tina gasped. "I couldn't move!"

Kate understood that too. "Sometimes that happens when we're scared."

Even as she spoke, Kate trembled. As though it were happening again, she saw the horse with Tina in its path.

Then Papa Nordstrom was there, trying to comfort both of them. Next to him stood Mama. Her face was white as she clung to the baby with one arm and hugged the girls with the other.

"Oh, Kate!" she exclaimed. "I saw you just as you ran for Tina." Mama bit her lip, unable to go on.

Behind Mama, Anders and Lars and Ben appeared, looking just as scared.

"You're a heroine!" Lars told Kate. Freckles surrounded his serious blue eyes.

"Yah, sure." Anders grinned. For once, he wasn't teasing.

A shudder ran through Kate's body. Then Ben reached out, took her hand, and helped her up. As she looked into his eyes, her uncle winked and said, "I don't know how you manage to find so much trouble!"

Kate knew he was trying to help her. She took one step and stopped. Her knees still felt weak.

Just then steam engine 328 came around the last curve. With squealing brakes the train known as the Blueberry Special came to a stop.

As the passengers stepped down, Kate searched each face. First came two salesmen, each carrying a suitcase with bold letters advertising their products. An older man with white hair was next. He stepped down, then turned back to help a lady wearing a long black coat.

Kate started forward. Could this be Grandpa and Grandma? But Mama stayed where she was, and Kate knew the couple had to be strangers.

Next came a young woman. A large feather curled over the brim of her hat and down along the side of her face. "Rose Marie!" someone called, and Kate saw the young man who met her.

Then the doorway was empty. A minute stretched out, seeming forever. Kate saw her mother's worried eyes.

Finally a family started down the steps. The man held a young girl. The woman clutched the hand of an older boy.

Mama looked relieved. "There are still more passengers." She edged closer to the train, but Ben hung back from the rest of the family.

He's worried, Kate thought. After stealing money from a shopkeeper in Sweden, Ben had disappeared. For some time no one in the family knew where he was.

Mama turned to Papa. "It's taking my parents a long time to get off," she said bravely.

Papa walked over to the conductor. "Do you have any more passengers?"

The conductor shook his head. "Grantsburg is the end of the line. Everyone is off."

"You're certain?"

"That's all the passengers we took on at Rush City." People coming from Minnesota changed trains at the small town seventeen miles away.

"There was no older Swedish couple?"

"Just the man and woman who got off." The conductor searched Papa's face. "I'm sorry."

Papa sighed. Slowly he turned toward Mama, as though wishing he didn't have to tell her.

Mama had already heard. "Where can they be?" she asked.

"I don't know," Papa answered. "Maybe they missed their train in New York. Or their train in St. Paul."

"Maybe, maybe!" Mama exclaimed. Her tall strong body sagged.

All week Kate had helped Mama clean and bake. Kate knew how much her mother had looked forward to seeing her parents. And now they were not here!

Papa led Mama back to the train station, and the others followed. Outside the door, Mama dropped weakly onto a bench.

"Maybe they'll send a message," Anders said. His thatch of blond hair no longer looked combed.

As though feeling hopeless, Mama shook her head. "They know we don't have a telephone. And there are only a few telephones in Grantsburg. How would they know who to call?"

"They could telegraph," Kate said, trying to sound more convincing than Anders.

Again Mama shook her head. "Grandpa and Grandma wouldn't know how to send a telegram."

"Someone will help them." Kate wished she believed her own words.

Just the same Mama looked hopeful. Then little Bernie stirred. Mama started rocking back and forth, but her thoughts seemed miles away.

By now the trainmen had separated the engine from the railroad cars. The engine backed onto the turntable—a short section of movable track less than a block from the station.

Suddenly Lars took off, running in that direction. At the turntable he talked with one of the trainmen. When the man nodded, Lars took a place alongside another boy. Together they leaned against a long lever, pushing. Slowly the engine swung around in a half circle until it faced the direction from which it came.

As the men started connecting cars to the engine once more, Papa sat down next to Mama. "I'll take the train to St. Paul," he said.

"Now?" Mama asked. "Without even an extra shirt?"

Papa nodded. "If I go home for anything, we'll lose a day of searching for Grandpa and Grandma. When they came through Ellis Island, someone probably pinned one piece of paper on Grandpa's coat and another on Grandma's."

"Yah, sure," Mama answered. "That's how good people in New York helped me onto the right train. All I had to do was point to the name on the paper."

She reached out her hand, and Papa took it in his. "It will be all right, Ingrid," he said.

"If I need to reach you, I'll send a message to Pastor Munson." The Minneapolis pastor had introduced Papa and Mama.

"I'll check there," Papa said. He looked up at Ben. "Why don't you come with me? You know how Grandpa and Grandma look."

The young man nodded. "I just hope that when we find them, they really want to see me!"

"They will," Mama promised.

When the conductor called, "All ah-booooaaaard!" Papa patted Mama's shoulder. He cupped his big hand around Bernie's little head, then said goodbye to each of them.

"Take good care of Mama, won't you?" he said to Kate. Over a year had passed since her widowed mother had married Papa Nordstrom. Mama and Kate had moved from Minneapolis to Windy Hill Farm.

Kate nodded, solemn with the responsibility of it. Then she watched her stepfather and uncle hurry toward the train. A moment later the conductor closed the door.

As the Blueberry Special chugged out of town, Mama lifted her chin and tried to smile. Yet she couldn't hold back her questions. "Where can my mama and papa be? What has happened to them?"

2

Surprise Journey

*I*n the middle of the night Kate woke to a steady pounding. At first she thought she was dreaming. Then, while still half asleep, she realized the noise was real. From somewhere below her—the kitchen perhaps—someone was knocking.

Still feeling confused, Kate slipped out of bed, grabbed her robe, and started for the stairs. It seemed that days instead of hours had passed since the trip from Grantsburg. Never had the road seemed so long, nor so sad.

Now as Kate hurried down the steps, Anders stepped into the hallway behind her. As they passed through the dining room, the pounding stopped. When they reached the kitchen, Mama stood in the doorway, talking to a man.

"Yah, yah, *tack*," she said. The Swedish word for thanks sounded like the tock of a clock. "Can you wait? We may need to answer."

As Mama turned from the door, a candle trembled in her hand. Kate took the candle from her and lit the kerosene lamp on the table.

Mama sank into her chair. "A telegram," she said, holding up an envelope. "It must be from Grandpa and Grandma."

With nervous fingers she pulled out a sheet of paper. Mama read the words aloud with the word *stop* where a period should be.

WE MISSED GETTING OFF AT RUSH CITY STOP
WE ARE IN DULUTH BUT MAMA IS LOST STOP
HELP ME FIND HER STOP
COME TO IMM—

Mama paused. Her English was good, but every now and then she had trouble reading.

Kate hurried around behind Mama and sounded out the word. "Imm-ah-grant. 'Come to immigrant room,' it says. They must have a special room for people coming to live in America."

Mama read on. "Union Dee-pot."

"Dee-poe," Kate pronounced. "The building where people wait for a train."

"Grandma is *lost*?" Mama asked. "If you ask me, both of them are lost. What does my papa mean?"

With a sinking feeling, Kate looked toward Anders. His blond hair lay this way and that. When their gaze met, Kate knew her brother felt just as worried as she did.

As if suddenly understanding the telegram, Mama groaned. "He means that Grandma has *disappeared*? Oh, how awful!"

Mama's eyes grew wet with tears. "My poor old mama, lost in a strange country. What could have happened to her?"

The man near the door shifted his feet. Mama glanced up. "Come, come. I forget my manners. Kate, please make him some coffee."

Kate hurried to the cookstove. Opening a stove lid, she dropped in firewood, then filled the pot with water and coffee. Quickly she sliced Mama's good bread and hurried to the cellar for cheese.

When Kate returned to the kitchen, Mama's hands were steady again. "You must go to Duluth, Anders. And Kate, you go with him. I will tell Grandpa you are coming."

Anders brought paper and pen and ink from the dining room.

With a careful hand Mama wrote her answer.

KATE AND ANDERS COMING ON FIRST TRAIN STOP
WILL HELP YOU FIND GRANDMA STOP

Her blue eyes wide with worry, Mama looked up. "Is that all I should say?"

"Tell him we'll come to the immigrant room," Anders said. "If he leaves there, we'll never find him."

Once more, the pen scratched. Then Mama wrote out another telegram asking Papa and Ben to come home. She folded the paper and tucked it inside an envelope.

"*Tack* for waiting," she said as she gave the man money for the telegrams.

Hearing Mama speak Swedish, Kate guessed how upset her mother really was.

As soon as the man finished eating, he hurried off. Through the closed door, Kate heard hoofbeats moving away in the distance.

Mama paid little attention. She was writing again.

"I want Erik to go with you," she said as she finished the note. "He'll take good care of you."

In spite of her worry about Grandma, Kate's temper flared. She tossed her long black braid over her shoulder.

I can take care of myself, she wanted to blurt out. But she didn't dare say it aloud. Mama might make her stay home.

"Erik has good common sense," Mama went on.

Sure, Kate thought. *Like I don't.* More than once, she'd rushed into trouble, drawn on by curiosity.

Thinking of Erik, she felt ashamed. Often he had helped her when she might have been seriously hurt. Besides that, he was a special friend.

Mama handed the note to Anders. "If Erik can go along, tell Lundgrens we'll pay for his ticket."

Already forgetting her resentment, Kate stared at Mama. Less than a year before, Erik's father had lost his farm to a dishonest person. Now the Lundgren family was starting over by renting the farm next to Windy Hill.

Erik seldom talked about it, but Kate knew his family had even less money than other farmers in the area. How could Mama remember something like that when she was so upset?

"If you hurry, you can make the early morning train," Mama said as Anders headed out the door barefoot. Whenever possible, Anders avoided shoes all summer long.

As Kate packed a battered suitcase, she heard the pounding of horse's hooves past the window. On his horse Wildfire, Anders would take no time at all to ride through the pasture and woods to Erik's house.

When Anders reappeared in the kitchen, Kate and Mama had filled a basket with food.

"Erik's brother John will take us," Anders said and left to pack his own suitcase.

"Do you have a clean shirt?" Mama asked when Anders returned to the kitchen.

Anders grinned. "I took Papa's good one. I'll look swell for the big city."

For the first time since learning her parents weren't on the train, Mama smiled. To Kate it seemed as though the sun had come out after a rain. Already Anders was over six feet tall. He was growing so fast that he fit into all of Papa's clothes.

"If we don't hear from you, we'll believe everything is going well," Mama said as Anders pulled on Papa's old boots. "No news is good news." She crossed to the cupboard.

Behind her back, Kate looked at Anders again. The worry she'd felt at the station in Grantsburg had returned. Like an ache it tightened her stomach. Would no news *really* be good news?

At the cupboard Mama set aside the sugar bowl and reached for the cup where she put her egg money. Carefully she counted out the change.

"I hope it's enough for three tickets," she said as she gave the coins to Anders. "Don't eat all your food at once. There might not be any money left over."

Then Erik was at the door. Like Anders, he was over six feet tall and broad-shouldered from farm work. But Erik's hair was brown instead of blond.

"Sit down," Mama told all of them as she hurried into the dining room. A moment later she returned, carrying the picture of her family.

"You need to know how my papa and mama look," she said to Erik as all of them gathered around the kitchen table.

Erik studied the picture, then passed it on to Anders. He, in turn, gave it to Kate.

Kate knew the photograph well. This time she looked at her grandparents in a new way. Mama's mother and father sat in the center, surrounded by Mama's five sisters and two brothers. The youngest brother was Ben at two years of age.

A sister held a framed photograph of Mama. "So I could still be part of the family," Mama often explained. Soon after coming to America, she'd had the photo of herself taken and sent to her parents.

Now Kate studied Grandpa's hands, his eyes and hair, and the shape of his chin. She tried to memorize each detail. But then she looked at her grandmother. *What if something terrible has happened? What if I come this close to knowing Grandma and never see her?*

Kate's Irish grandparents also lived across the ocean. She had never met even one of them. When children at school talked about their own grandparents, Kate always wished she could know hers.

"What will Grandpa and Grandma be like?" she had asked Mama at least a hundred times.

Each time Mama smiled. "You will love them. And they will love you."

Now Kate set the picture down on the table.

"When you get to Duluth, stay together," Mama said. "Don't take any chances."

Kate saw her brother's grin. She and Anders had heard Mama's words of warning more than once.

"You will need wisdom," Mama said and cleared her throat. She stood up and took the big family Bible from the shelf.

As she thought about leaving, Kate felt scared. *I've never been away from home on such a long trip.*

The next moment she felt excited. *What will it be like?* Duluth was a big city. A busy port on Lake Superior, the largest fresh water lake in the world. Often she'd heard about Duluth, Minnesota, and its sister city, Superior, Wisconsin. Together they were called the Twin Ports.

Mama opened the Bible and turned to the first chapter in the book of James. She read the fifth verse slowly, her finger pointing to each word. " 'If any of you lack wisdom, let him ask of God, that giveth to all men liberally. . . . ' "

Mama glanced up. "That means God will give you all the wisdom you need."

She continued reading. " 'But let him ask in faith, nothing wavering. For he that wavereth is like a wave of the sea driven with the wind and tossed.' "

Ask in faith? What does that mean? Kate wondered.

Mama prayed then, and Kate forgot her question. She wanted to hang on to each of Mama's words.

"Heavenly Father, we ask thee to watch over Kate and Anders and Erik and keep them safe. Help them to find Grandma—" Mama's voice broke off.

"We ask for your wisdom," said Erik, taking up the prayer.

Startled, Kate opened her eyes. Anders was also watching Erik. For some time Kate had known that Erik believed in God. Yet he was usually quiet about his faith. What had caused him to speak now?

After a moment, Mama went on, but her voice still trembled. "Lord, I ask thee to hold my mama in thy arms, and my papa too. In thy name I ask thee to bring all of us safely together again. Ah-men."

"Ah-men," echoed the others.

As Kate slipped out into the night, she still felt the warmth of her mother's hug. Erik's brother, John, waited on the trail that passed the farm. When he saw Kate, he jumped down from the wagon. Taking her hand, he helped Kate up to the high spring seat, then climbed up beside her.

Anders and Erik settled the suitcases and basket of food in the back. Erik scrambled up to Kate's other side. Anders climbed into the wagon bed, walked forward, and sat down against the side of the wagon just behind Erik.

A kerosene farm lantern hung from a ring in the harness between the two horses. John flicked the reins, and Queen and Prince started past the log barn.

On the long trail to the main road, Kate looked up at John. He was six years older and even taller than Erik. His face and hands were bronzed by the sun.

"Thanks for taking us to town," Kate said shyly. She had never really talked to John before. Always she saw him from a distance, as some grown-up person she didn't know.

John grinned. "My pleasure."

In the moonlight his smile flashed. He looked happier tonight than the last time Kate had seen him. At a box social at Spirit Lake School he and Ben had bid against each other.

It had been a hard battle with the bid going to an unbelievable five dollars. John had lost out, and Ben got to eat with Miss Sundquist, the teacher. John hadn't enjoyed losing.

Now as they rounded a bend in the trail, he suddenly leaned against Kate. She in turn fell against Erik. Erik grabbed the seat.

"John!" Erik complained.

"Move over, little brother," John drawled. "You're taking too much room."

Kate snickered and saw red creep into Erik's neck.

"Good thing I'm along to protect you in the dark," John told Kate.

"We've always managed to protect Kate before," Erik said stiffly.

"But we have to admit, it's a mighty big job," Anders joined in.

Kate ignored him. Turning slightly, she kept her back toward Erik and talked only to John.

"I'm old enough to take care of myself," she said sweetly.

"That so?" John replied. "I thought all young ladies like being taken care of."

This time it was Kate's turn to feel embarrassed.

John talked all the way to Grantsburg. For eleven miles he

ignored Erik and Anders as though he and Kate were alone.

As they neared the town, the sky gradually grew light. A soft breeze stirred the hair around Kate's face. Above the clopping of the horses, Kate heard the birds begin to sing.

On the outskirts of Grantsburg she also heard a long whistle.

"That's the train coming in!" she exclaimed. "We're going to miss it!"

John slapped the reins. The wagon jerked forward.

Again John slapped the reins, and the horses broke into a run. Down the main street of town they tore, with the wagon swinging from side to side. Feeling as if she were going to bounce out, Kate clung to the edge of the seat.

3

Discovery at the Depot

*A*t the station, John cried, "Whoa!" Next to the platform he pulled the horses to a stop.

Kate jumped down. As she raced for the train, the last passenger climbed aboard.

The conductor swung his arm, signaling the engineer. The engineer released the brake, and steam poured out along the track.

"Wait!" Kate shouted.

The conductor saw her and waved. "Jump on!"

As the train started to move, he helped Kate up the steps. The boys, with the suitcases and basket of food, were close behind.

An instant later, the train picked up speed. Safely inside the door, Kate caught her breath. The boys crowded in behind her.

As Anders paid the conductor for the first part of their trip, Kate walked forward into the passenger car. Soon the Hickerson Roller Mill slipped past the window. Then the Grantsburg Brick Factory with its kilns and yard fell into the distance.

Kate dropped into an empty seat. Erik and Anders put away the suitcases, then sat down in the seat facing her.

As soon as she pushed the hair out of her eyes, Kate was ready to tease. "Glad you boys managed to get on."

"Glad you let us carry everything while you ran," Anders told her.

Erik simply looked at her.

"You sure were quiet on the trip in," Kate told him, her voice as sweet as she could make it.

"Big brothers are a pain!" Erik growled.

"Well, I certainly agree with you there." Glancing toward Anders, Kate lifted an eyebrow.

Anders scowled at her. "You made a fool of yourself!"

"A fool?" Kate asked lightly. She flipped her long braid over her shoulder.

"A fool," Erik answered. "John is six years older than you."

"Really?" Kate offered her nicest smile. It was fun teasing Erik. At school her rival Maybelle was usually around, always trying to flirt with him.

"Not much more than the difference in age between Papa and Mama," Kate said.

"That's different!" Erik exclaimed. "They're older!"

He leaned back, as though telling himself he wouldn't let Kate get the best of him.

"You're just used to having me around," Kate said. "I didn't think you'd mind having me sit next to your handsome brother."

An angry light settled in Erik's eyes. "I don't," he said. He turned and stared out the window.

Anders studied the back of his friend's head as if seeing Erik for the first time. When Anders finally looked at Kate, he gave her a long slow wink.

Kate giggled, but Erik pretended not to hear. Seventeen miles later, he was still staring out the window when the engine stopped alongside the Rush City, Minnesota, depot.

From Rush City a train went north to Duluth or south to Minneapolis and St. Paul. Inside the station, Kate, Anders, and Erik settled down to wait. Kate lifted the cover over Mama's basket and took out breakfast. Already the pint jars of milk were starting to grow warm.

When they finished eating, Anders bought tickets for the next part of their journey. He came away from the window looking worried. "Mama knew what she was talking about. We haven't got much money left."

"Maybe we'll find Grandma right away, so we can go home," Kate answered. Yet she sounded more hopeful than she felt.

"I bought round-trip tickets," her brother said. "At least we have a way to get back. But let's take it easy on the food."

Kate laughed.

Anders grinned. "Guess I just need to talk to myself." It was no secret that he always ate more than everyone else.

In the middle of the morning they boarded another train and settled back for a long ride. The one hundred miles to Duluth would take almost four hours.

At first Kate looked out the windows. Here and there, between the trees, lay scattered farms. Whenever they came to a small town, the conductor called out the name, and the train ground to a halt.

As time grew long, Kate began reading the signs posted along the sides of the car next to the ceiling. When she'd read every one, she stared out the window again.

No matter how hard she tried to think about other things, she couldn't push her worry aside. Behind everything she said or did, her concern about Grandma was there. *She doesn't even know Ben is here, living with us.*

When Ben reached America, he had found a job and repaid the money he stole. From the shopkeeper Grandpa and Grandma learned that Ben planned to go to Minnesota.

Kate thought back to the letter in which her grandparents told about their plans to come to America. "Will you help us look for Ben?" they asked. "We cannot die without finding him and making things right between us. We want to tell him that we love him still."

By the time Mama received the letter, it was too late for a letter to reach Grandma and Grandpa. They had no idea that Ben had come to Windy Hill Farm.

Now Kate wondered, *What if we don't find Grandma? Will*

Ben always blame himself? Will he feel it's his fault?

Kate turned to Anders. "When Grandpa says *lost*, what do you think he means?"

Her brother shrugged. "Hard to tell. We don't know how much English he knows. Probably not much."

"But someone must have helped him," Erik said. He seemed to have forgotten his anger at Kate. "Your grandpa probably didn't send that telegram by himself."

"That's right!" Kate answered. She herself had hoped that Grandpa would get that kind of help. In the excitement of the middle-of-the-night telegram, she had forgotten.

Now she thought back. When Ben first came to America, he had known only the English he learned on the ship. Was Grandpa the same?

"There has to be someone in the immigrant room." Erik seemed to have thought it through. "Someone who understood what your grandpa was saying in Swedish."

Kate nodded. "And that person knew how to translate—to change Grandpa's Swedish into English."

"Then *lost* does mean *lost*," Erik said. "Just like it would if we used the word. It has to mean separated from Grandpa."

Kate felt sure Erik was right, but his words made her feel worse, not better. For a long time she was silent, just thinking about Grandma. What would it be like being all alone in a strange country?

And why did it happen? Both Mama and Papa had talked about the way kind people showed immigrants the right train. But every now and then a mean person tried to get the best of immigrants who didn't understand what was going on.

That's what really bothered Kate. "Why did Grandma and Grandpa get separated?"

Anders shrugged.

"We don't know either, Kate," Erik said quietly.

"There must be something really wrong."

When Kate saw Erik's eyes, she knew. He had already decided the same thing.

———

Brakes squealed. Cars clanked together as the train came to a stop in Duluth. Kate and the boys were first down the steps. As they followed a long aisle between tracks, billows of smoke from departing engines darkened the air.

Around them, people hurried to their trains, walking as if they knew where they were going. Many of those coming off the trains seemed more uncertain, the way Kate felt. She wished it didn't all seem so overwhelming.

As Erik led them around a gigantic engine, Kate saw a brick building. A woman stood near the doorway, guiding people up the stairs.

"You want the immigrant room?" she asked when Anders explained. "Halfway between here and the main floor."

When Kate found the room, clusters of people blocked the doorway. She stopped, wondering how to slip through. Then a man stepped aside, creating a narrow path. Anders and Erik followed close behind.

Just inside the room, Kate found a small place to stand and look around.

The room was about forty feet long and at least thirty feet wide. Wooden benches with iron armrests lined the yellow tile walls. More benches filled the area in the center of the room. Wherever Kate looked, there were people.

Some sat quietly, waiting, like the old woman wearing a long black skirt. The shawl over her head extended halfway down her back.

In a corner a man lay on the floor, sound asleep. Others slept in the benches, sitting up.

Still other people looked restless. Babies cried. Two boys tried to chase each other, but their parents stopped them. A young man walked up and down the narrow aisles, moving wherever he could find space. Kate wondered if he wanted to stretch his legs after the fifty-hour train ride from New York.

Close at hand, two women threw their arms around each other in happy reunion. Were they sisters who hadn't seen each other for years?

As the noise rose around her, Kate tried to pick out the languages. Many of the people seemed to come from Sweden or Norway. Kate recognized the sound. But were there immigrants from Germany and Poland—perhaps Denmark, Scotland, and Italy, as well?

When she lived in Minneapolis Kate had heard various languages, but now she couldn't sort them out. A mixture of many voices—some happy, some tired—surrounded her, as though coming in waves. After being up most of the night, Kate felt light-headed, as if the noises would drown her.

Again she felt overwhelmed. It wasn't difficult to guess how Grandma could become separated from Grandpa.

"There must be hundreds of people," Kate said, turning back to Anders and Erik. "All jammed into this one room! How will we ever find Grandpa?"

"Let's split up," answered Erik. "We can each search a third of the room."

Kate took the side closest to the entry. A large sign posted on the tile wall said FINNS! The picture showed work in a logging camp. But Kate couldn't read the words below.

Large immigrant trunks, suitcases, and boxes jammed the space between benches. A little girl peeked around her mother's skirt. A baby slept on his mother's shoulder.

Starting at the row next to the wall, Kate studied the face of every person. She saw tired faces, discouraged faces. Many of the immigrants looked up as she passed. The light in their eyes told Kate they hoped she was a relative here to meet them.

Toward the back corner Kate came to a long line of people standing outside a door. On the upper half of the frosted window was a single word: SHOWER.

"Is that the bathroom?" Kate asked a woman waiting in the line.

Palms up, the woman shrugged.

"Toilet?" Kate asked.

This time the woman understood. "Yah."

"That's the only bathroom for all these people?" Again Kate's English was too much for the woman.

Then another woman, this one holding a pot of coffee, turned toward Kate. "There is only one toilet," she said. "And one shower."

"For all these people?" Kate asked.

The woman sighed. "One family uses the room at a time. It will be a long wait."

Kate swallowed hard. She stretched out her hand toward the crowds around her. "How many people—"

She broke off, but the woman seemed to understand what Kate was asking.

"Often we have two thousand immigrants pass through the depot in a week. Some leave right away. Others wait overnight or a couple of days until relatives come to meet them."

Nearby, a young boy started to cry. His mother reached out and drew the three- or four-year-old to her.

Kate turned back to the woman. "And you? Who are you?"

"Mrs. Barclay. I am one of the women who helps immigrants. We come from churches and the YWCA."

She held out a tray filled with cups and rolls. "We bring coffee and help people find rooms and jobs."

"My grandpa is here somewhere," Kate said. "His name is Peter Lindblom. White hair, blue eyes, a black coat and trousers, Mama thinks. Have you seen him?"

As Mrs. Barclay looked around, Kate sensed the difficulty of what she asked. Everywhere there was black clothing.

Yet as Mrs. Barclay moved away, she promised, "I'll keep my eyes open."

Kate started down the second row of benches, gazing into every face. More than once she saw faded blue eyes. Always Kate gave that face a second look, hoping to find the man in the picture.

She had worked her way toward the middle of the room when she heard Erik's voice. "Kate!"

Above the heads he motioned, telling her to come over. Beside Erik stood an older man, leaning against a cane.

Kate's heart leaped. For a moment she stood still. *Is this my grandfather?*

4

Gold Coins

$\mathcal{T}$he man wore a long black coat, open now in the heat of the room. Like countless other men, he had black trousers with suspenders. The face was that in Mama's picture.

My grandpa, Kate told herself. For a moment she treasured the thought. *My very own grandpa!* Never before had a grandparent seemed real to her.

Then Kate hurried around the benches and clusters of people. Just before reaching Erik, she stopped, unable to go a step farther.

The man straightened. He was shorter than Erik and his hair was gray, not white. His eyes looked younger than his years. Around the outer edges were the wrinkles of laugh lines.

Laugh lines? Kate wondered. *In spite of your hard life?* She had expected him to look stern, and it surprised her.

Then the man stretched out his hand. As Kate took it, he dropped his cane and closed his other hand over hers.

"Grandpa?" Kate asked shyly, wishing she knew more Swedish. Her Daddy O'Connell had been Irish, and Kate and Mama spoke English with him.

"Peter Lindblom," Erik said quietly.

Grandpa stood without speaking, his eyes searching out every detail about Kate. At last he cleared his throat. *"Lilla flicka!"*

Lee-la flick-ah, Kate thought. *Little girl.*

"It is good to look upon my granddaughter."

As Erik translated, Grandpa's hands tightened, still holding Kate's. "Your black hair, the color of your blue eyes—they must come from your father. But you look like my Emma. My Emma when she was your age."

"Like Grandma?" Kate asked as soon as Erik translated.

"Like your grandma."

Tears welled up in Kate's eyes. *But will I ever see her?*

A look of pain crossed the old man's face, then was gone. "Now that you are here, we will find her."

"You met my friend Erik?" Kate asked. Gone was their argument on the train. It felt good to introduce him.

Kate wondered at the pride she felt about having Erik as a friend. Grandpa shook his hand, and Kate looked around for Anders.

Her brother had seen them. He was weaving his way around the groups of people. When he reached Grandpa, Anders towered above him by three or four inches.

Grandpa looked him up and down. "My Ingrid's new son," he said, "and now, my grandson." He offered his hand.

As Anders took it, Grandpa spoke again. "Welcome to our family."

Anders blinked, as though surprised at the warmth of Grandpa's greeting. He pumped Grandpa's hand, then picked up the forgotten cane. With surprising gentleness he gave it to Grandpa.

The old man limped as he walked back to his large trunk. Bending as if his knee were stiff, Grandpa picked up a small wooden carving. He held it out to Kate.

"Only now I have finished it," he said.

Kate looked down to a carving of an older woman. With a scarf around her head and wearing a long skirt and apron, the woman sat on a three-legged stool. In one hand she held what seemed to be three tiny knitting needles, crossed to form a triangle. In the other hand she held a fourth needle, as though she were knitting mittens.

"That is my Emma," Grandpa said softly.

"Grandma?" Kate asked as she took the carving.

He nodded. "Grandma."

"This is how she looks?"

Grandpa nodded.

With a careful finger Kate touched the tiny face, the hollows in her cheeks. The woman's hair was drawn back, almost hidden by the shawl over her head.

She was so near. And now so far away. Where can she be?

Kate wiped a tear away and struggled to speak. "Will you tell us how Grandma got lost?"

With Erik translating, the story came out. Grandpa and Grandma had missed their change of trains at Rush City. When they reached Duluth, they discovered they were in the wrong place. Grandma carried most of their money in a large cloth bag with two wooden handles. She took out some of the money and gave it to Grandpa. He left to buy tickets for the return trip to Rush City.

As though unable to go on, Grandpa stopped speaking. Finally he said, "When I came back, my Emma was gone."

"Gone?" Kate asked.

"Gone." Grandpa looked around the room. "Nowhere."

"You have no idea where she went?"

"Someone must have seen her take out the money." Grandpa sank down on the nearby bench. "That coat! That's what brought all the trouble!"

"What coat?" Kate dropped to her knees, directly in front of him. "What do you mean?"

With his elbows on his knees, Grandpa held his head in his hands. His shoulders shook as if he were weeping. Yet no tears came.

Reaching out, Kate patted Grandpa's shoulder. It felt strange, comforting this man she barely knew. Yet somehow his weeping reminded her of Mama.

"What do you mean, Grandpa?" Kate asked again, and Erik translated.

Grandpa looked up. "My Emma looked like a queen in that coat."

"A queen?" Kate wondered if the strain of the long trip had been too much for him.

Grandpa nodded. "Like your mama, Emma is tall. She stands straight. Like a queen she looked in that coat."

Anders knelt down next to Kate. Looking into Grandpa's eyes, Anders spoke in Swedish. "We don't understand. If we're going to help you, we have to understand."

"Yah, certainly." Grandpa took a deep breath. "I must not carry on so."

He drew himself up. "On the way to our ship, we stopped in Sweden to visit Emma's sister. In the depot I saw a young boy wander away from his mother. He started across the tracks in front of a train. I ran out, snatched up the child, and brought him to safety."

"You saved the boy's life?" Anders asked.

Grandpa nodded. "His parents said, 'How can we thank you?' They seemed very rich and wanted to give us money.

" 'No, no, we will not take money,' I said. 'We are glad the little one is all right.'

" 'You are going to America?' the mother asked. She looked at Emma. 'You will need a warm coat for crossing the cold ocean.' She took off her coat and put it on Emma. She took Emma's old coat and put it on herself.

"Then the mother pushed back the shawl on Emma's head. She took a jeweled comb from her hair and set it in Emma's. My Emma looked like a queen, I tell you. Straight and tall she stood, like a queen.

" 'No, no,' we said again, but they would not listen. Instead, the woman held out some red yarn. 'I just bought this. You can make gifts for your family in America.' She put the beautiful yarn in Grandma's big bag.

"Grandma shook her head. 'It is too much.'

"The woman took Grandma's hands and looked into her eyes.

'There is nothing we can give that is worth the life of our son.'

"Her husband shook my hand again. Then we climbed aboard our train. We sailed from Göteborg, a city on the west coast of Sweden. From there we took a ship to Hull in England. We took another train across the country to Liverpool.

"It wasn't until we boarded our ship to America that Grandma reached down into the very bottom of her bag. There she found some gold coins—English money the father probably got when traveling. He must have slipped them into Grandma's bag as we talked.

"When we reached America, we changed some of the gold coins into silver dollars and came here. A kind lady who works in this room helped me send a telegram to you."

Grandpa ran his fingers through his hair. "It's the coat!" he said again.

"The coat caused all your trouble?" Kate still didn't understand.

"The coat had fur, going this way and that." Grandpa pointed in two directions. He shook his head at the thought of such a use of money.

"The coat is *fur*?" Kate asked. "And the fur goes another way around the bottom of the coat?" Once she had seen such a coat with a fur border around the hem. It belonged to a wealthy lady in Minneapolis.

Grandpa nodded. "The lady wanted to be kind. But often Grandma said, 'This coat is not like me. This is not what I am.' She did not feel good wearing something so expensive. And now, it has caused this trouble!"

"Someone thinks you are rich," Kate said.

"Yah. Someone thinks we are *very* rich."

A hard knot settled in Kate's stomach. For the first time she understood the full meaning of Grandpa's story. "You think someone took Grandma to get her money?"

Discouragement filled Grandpa's eyes. "Bad things will happen if we don't find Emma soon."

Kate glanced at Erik and Anders. The look on their faces told her all she needed to know. Grandpa was probably right.

Kate took her grandfather's hand. If only she could give him hope.

"Grandpa, we need to know some other things." It was Erik who asked now, sounding as if Grandpa were his own grandfather. Erik spoke softly, as though not wanting to frighten the old man more. "What else was Grandma wearing?"

"A skirt," Grandpa answered.

"The color?" Kate asked.

"A black skirt."

Kate glanced around. Nearly every woman in the room wore a long black skirt.

"She had gray hair?" Kate asked, and Anders translated.

"It is white now."

"Is there something that would make Grandma look different from other women?" Kate asked.

"The coat," Grandpa said grimly. Then he was silent, as though thinking. Finally he pointed to his head. "Waves."

"Waves?" Not even Erik understood. "Are you talking about the ocean?"

For the first time Grandpa smiled. He touched his head again, this time at the two sides.

"Ahhh!" Understanding dawned on Kate. She turned to Anders and Erik. "You know how women pull their hair straight back in a bun? But Mama's hair waves on both sides of her head. Grandma's hair must be the same way."

Erik translated, and Grandpa nodded. He held his hand above his head.

Anders spoke quickly in Swedish, then explained to Kate. "Grandma is taller than he is."

"And her face like this." Grandpa took the carving from Kate. His hands were rough from farm work, but gentle, as he touched the small wooden face.

"Can we take this with us to show people what she looks like?" Kate asked.

"Yah, sure. I started to carve it on the ship. Ever since Grandma disappeared, I have worked. I wanted to give a picture."

Again Kate wondered, *How can we give him hope?*

Suddenly she remembered. "Ben is here," she said. "Ben is living with us."

"Yah?" asked Grandpa when Erik translated. "Ben is *here*?"

"He came a short time ago," Kate answered.

"Ben lives with *you*?" Grandpa looked as if he could not believe her words.

Kate nodded.

"He is a good boy?"

Kate nodded. "He is a good boy."

"I will see him again?" Grandpa asked.

"And Grandma will see him again," Kate promised. "We will find her."

"Such a miracle—that Ben is here." Grandpa shook his head as though unable to take it in. But hope lit his eyes. "I can hardly wait to tell my Emma."

Kate turned to Anders and Erik. "Let's try to find someone who has been here as long as Grandpa. Maybe there's a person who saw something Grandpa didn't."

Anders explained to Grandpa.

"I wish I could help you," Grandpa answered. "I fell on the ship and hurt my knee. When I got here, I walked outside to look for my Emma. That's all the farther I could go."

He returned the carving to Kate. She and Anders and Erik started their search by talking with people near Grandpa.

"How long have you been here?" they asked first. When they needed to, Erik or Anders spoke in Swedish. When that didn't help, they moved on to someone else.

Often Kate held out the small wood carving. Always the immigrants tried to be helpful. Yet one by one, they shook their head. No one had seen someone who looked like Grandma.

Finally, three rows away and near the door to the stairs, they found a man who spoke English. "Yup! I've been here since yesterday, waiting for my relatives to come in from the Iron Range."

Kate knew he was talking about the mines in northeastern Minnesota. She watched as he turned the carving over in his hands, then passed it back to Kate.

"White hair, you say? Tall for a woman." He stroked his chin, black with whiskers from not shaving. "Yup, I saw her. I'm sure of it. About this time yesterday."

"She was by herself?"

The man shook his head. "The man with her was tall. Mustache that came down over his upper lip, as though it needed trimming. The man and the lady just didn't fit together. That's why I remember. That and the fur coat."

"Can you think of anything more?" Kate asked. The man's description of the person with Grandma didn't make her feel better, but at least they had some clues.

"I heard the man talk to her. He said, 'Your husband is hurt. I'll take you to him.' He was rushing her a bit. They headed out that door."

He tipped his head toward the exit leading to the stairs. "That's the last I saw them."

5

New Clues

$\mathcal{T}$he last you saw them?" Kate asked. She didn't like the sound of those words.

"Sorry, little lady. If I had known—" the man broke off. "Is there something wrong?"

Kate nodded, the ache within her growing. "Something is terribly wrong. My grandmother is missing."

"Let's go upstairs," Erik said. "Maybe we'll find out more."

Anders shook his head. "I'm going to stay with Grandpa. I'll make sure we don't lose *him*."

Kate and Erik made their way between the groups of people. Outside the immigrant room, they started up the stairs. The half flight of steps brought them into a huge hall. On two sides of the room were large brick fireplaces. On the third wall was a lunch counter and a place for selling tickets.

Rows of benches filled the large open space. Here, too, people hurried back and forth. Yet this waiting room was so much larger than the immigrant room that it did not seem crowded.

Kate tipped back her head to look up at the wood beams of the ceiling, far above. "How high do you think it is?"

"The ceiling?" Erik grinned. "If Anders was here, he'd call you curious Kate."

Just the same, he also gazed upward. "At least eighty feet high, I think. Close to ninety. I'm over six feet tall. If you stacked thirteen or fourteen of me on top of each other, it'd be about right."

As Kate looked around at the great number of people, she wondered where to start asking questions. "If we go up and down the rows, we'll be here all night."

She looked toward the large windows on the fourth side of the room. The long shadows of late afternoon fell across the sidewalk.

"Let's think," Erik said. "If the man told Grandma he's taking her to see Grandpa, where would he go?"

"Away from here," Kate said. She headed for the large doors leading to the street. Beyond the covered entrance, a long line of drivers waited with their horses and buggies.

"Do you think all these people have someone coming in on a train?" Erik asked.

Kate shook her head. "They're men driving hacks—horses and buggies for hire. If it's like Minneapolis, they'll take you wherever you want to go."

Kate grinned. "For a price, of course."

"Then that's where we start." Erik went to the head of the line. Holding up Grandpa's carving, he asked, "Have you seen a woman who looks like this? She probably wore a fur coat."

One man after another shook his head. Finally they found a hack driver who said, "You know, a man was here yesterday morning, asking the same questions. Are you from that family?"

"What do you mean?" Kate asked.

"A rich gent pulled up right behind me. Black suit, gold watch chain across his vest, fine carriage and all. His driver hopped down and held the horses while the man went into the depot.

"While the driver waited, another man came over to talk. Mean-looking man. Mean eyes, like he was angry, or holding a grudge. The driver didn't want to talk to him."

"Did you hear what they said?" Erik asked.

"Nope! When the rich gent came back out the door, the man slipped around to the other side of the carriage. The gent told his driver, 'My parents aren't here. I don't know what happened to them.' Then he asked us questions, just like you did. Said he'd brought his mother and father over from Sweden, but they hadn't come in."

"Did you know any of the people?" Erik asked.

The hack driver shook his head. "The gent had a pair of high-stepping blacks. That's all I can tell you. But maybe someone else will know more."

Erik and Kate went on to the two remaining drivers. By the time they came to the end of the line, dusk had settled over the city. Along the sidewalk, street lights cast a soft glow.

When they questioned the last man without learning anything more, Kate groaned. "Oh, Erik, what are we going to do?"

Turning, she looked back at the Union Depot with its light colored brick and green slate roof. On either side of the entrance two large round towers seemed to stand guard.

"I wish those towers could talk," Kate said. "When we prayed with Mama, you asked for wisdom. But how will we know if we have it?"

Erik shrugged. "Maybe if things fall into place—if God gives us special help in figuring things out."

"Like what?" Worry nibbled away at Kate's insides. As she twisted the end of her braid, she wished she knew more about following God's guidance.

Erik leaned against a post as he thought about it. "Maybe we'll just know something—really know it, I mean. Or maybe one of us will have a thought that's so real it's almost like hearing a voice inside."

Kate was curious. "Are there other ways I can know?"

"Lots of 'em. You might have a nudge to do something—something good, I mean. You might think, 'I ought to do that.' Or you can have a nudge to *not* do something that would hurt you."

Kate looked at Erik with respect. "How did you learn things like that?"

Erik straightened. "My dad lost our farm because he trusted the wrong person—a man who was out to take everything we had. I started wondering if there were ways God would help me when I didn't know what to do."

Moments later, a driver pulled up at the end of the line. Erik hurried over to him. Once again he held up the carving.

"Sure, and I saw her," the man answered. "A lady with white hair. Looked very upset."

"Was someone with her?"

"Aye, a tall man wearing swell clothes. Bow tie. Smoked a cigar. Asked me to take them to St. Luke's Hospital. Still, and if it wasn't a wee bit strange."

"Strange?" Kate asked.

"At the hospital they got down. The man paid me, and they started toward the door. I drove off, but then I looked back. Instead of going inside, the man led the lady over to another hack. The man had a strong hold on the lady's arm."

"Like he was forcing her into the buggy?" Erik asked.

The driver pushed back his hat, scratched his balding head. "Maybe so. I thought he was holding her up. You know, like giving help. Now that I think of it. . . ." His voice trailed off.

"Do you know who the next driver was?"

"Aye, it was my friend Tony!"

"Where did he take them?" Kate asked quickly.

"Saw 'em start up the hill." The driver tipped his head toward the steep bluff above Union Depot. "Crossed over Superior Street. Don't know where they went from there. Maybe Duluth Heights. Maybe not."

"Is Tony around now?" Kate asked.

"Nope! Just two minutes ago I saw him take on a fancy man and his wife. Heard him give an address up the North Shore a ways. He won't be back tonight."

Filled with disappointment, Kate stepped away from the buggy. But Erik moved closer. "Will Tony come here in the morning?"

"More than likely. He owns a team of big bay horses. I'll tell him you need him. Where can he find you?"

Kate turned to Erik and found him looking at her. Soon it would be dark, and they had no place to go.

"Right here, I guess," Kate answered, her voice small.

Like a picture laid out before her, Kate remembered the kitchen at Windy Hill Farm. She smelled the bread coming out of the oven, saw the candles Mama put in the window when someone was away from home. In that moment Kate wished she could walk through that door.

"We'll be in the IMMIGRANT ROOM," Erik told the hack driver, sounding as if he, too, would like to be home.

Kate and Erik went back inside the depot. As they started down the stairs, Kate thought about all the immigrants who passed that way each day. *For now this room is their home. A stopping place in a long journey. A shelter—a place of new beginnings.*

Outside the door, Kate turned to Erik. "What should we tell Grandpa?"

Erik's eyes looked troubled. "I don't know."

"He's an old man. He doesn't look very strong."

Erik shook his head. "No, Kate, he's very strong."

Erik opened the door, and Kate felt relieved. He wouldn't give her time to decide.

When they found Grandpa and Anders, the old man pulled himself to his feet. He leaned on his cane, as though wanting to take any news standing up.

Erik spoke to him in Swedish. As Grandpa listened, the hand holding his cane trembled. Yet he nodded. "She is still alive. I know it. She is still alive."

"How do you know, Grandpa?" Kate asked.

The old man rested his hand on his chest. "I know it here. Peace—peace I feel. Yah, she is alive." Backing into the bench, he sat down.

Kate looked at Erik. "You are right," she said quietly. "He is very strong."

As she sat down next to Grandpa, Kate heard a voice from behind. "Coffee, anyone?"

Turning around, Kate saw Mrs. Barclay, the woman she had met earlier.

"You found your grandfather!" Mrs. Barclay held out a cup of coffee.

Kate passed the coffee and introduced him. "My grandpa, Peter Lindblom." Then she explained. "My grandmother is lost!"

When Kate finished the story of what had happened, Mrs. Barclay set down her tray. "We must get help! Stay right here."

She hurried through the crowd to the doorway. Minutes later, she returned, bringing along a policeman. "This is Sergeant Holmquist," Mrs. Barclay explained.

Quickly Anders and Erik told the officer what had happened. The sergeant spoke to Grandpa in Swedish, and Erik translated for Kate.

"Where did you search?" the officer asked.

"I went up the stairs to the large room," Grandpa answered. "I went outside and looked around. But it was no use.

"A lady helped me send a telegram. These good children came. They are my grandchildren." Grandpa waved his hand, including even Erik.

When the sergeant finished asking questions, he promised he would get more men to help him. Then he asked, "Where can I find you?"

"Right here," Grandpa answered. "I'll stay until you find my Emma."

Mrs. Barclay leaned forward and started speaking to Grandpa in another language.

"She must be Norwegian," Erik whispered to Kate. "I can understand what she's saying. She told Grandpa, 'Come to my house.' "

Grandpa shook his head. "No, no, it is too much."

"We have an Immigrant House," Mrs. Barclay explained. "A place where immigrants stay until they find work and a place to live. But it is full."

As Erik translated for Kate, Mrs. Barclay went on. "We have boardinghouses—large buildings where people rent a room for a week or month at a time. They are also full, and so are the hotels. Many, many people come here for work—for the mines, the logging, and the fishing. Our city is growing very fast."

Grandpa looked embarrassed. "I have only a few small coins. My money is with Emma."

"The children need a place to stay," answered Mrs. Barclay. "Especially Kate."

Grandpa looked at his granddaughter. "Yah," he said finally. "For Kate I go with you. *Tack, tack.*"

Mrs. Barclay nodded, accepting his thanks.

"Where do you live?" Sergeant Holmquist asked, and Mrs. Barclay gave him an address.

The sergeant turned back to Grandpa. "We'll look for Tony. I'll let you know whatever I learn."

As soon as Mrs. Barclay could leave, Anders grabbed the handle on one side of Grandpa's large trunk. Erik took hold of the other handle. Both of the boys were used to farm work and lifted the heavy trunk as if it were no effort at all.

Carrying the trunk between them, they started out of the immigrants' waiting room. Kate followed with Grandpa. He walked slowly, leaning heavily upon his cane.

At the top of the stairs the boys set the trunk down. Anders hurried back to help Grandpa up the steps.

As Kate watched her grandfather, her throat tightened. How much of Grandpa's weakness came from his fall on the ship? How much had come because of his great worry about Grandma?

Outside the depot, Mrs. Barclay signaled two hack drivers. Grandpa, Mrs. Barclay, and Anders went in the first buggy. Kate, Erik, and the trunk followed in the next.

"Will Grandpa ever see Grandma again?" Kate asked the minute she and Erik were alone.

For a moment Erik hesitated. Then he answered, "I want to believe that he will."

Kate tried to smile, but found it impossible. Instead, her throat tightened with tears.

"Will I ever meet Grandma?" Kate asked when she could speak. "I missed her by so little!"

"You will see her." Erik sounded as if there were no doubt about it.

"Will I ever get to know her?"

"You will get to know her."

As silent as spring rain, Kate's tears spilled over. She felt embarrassed but couldn't seem to stop crying. "How do you know?"

"I'm not sure I can explain it," Erik said slowly. "I guess I'm like Grandpa. He calls it peace."

By the time the hack driver stopped in front of Mrs. Barclay's house, anger had replaced Kate's tears. "How can a man be so terrible to a grandmother? What do you think is happening to her right now?"

6

Strange Hideaway

*E*rik didn't answer her question. Kate had the feeling he didn't want to say what he thought.

Mrs. Barclay's house was partway up the steep bluff that rose above downtown Duluth. Tall and narrow, the house seemed to grow out of the hillside. At one side of the front was a turret, a small tower at the corner of the house. Like the larger turrets on the Union Depot, it had a pointed roof.

Mrs. Barclay settled Grandpa into a second-floor bedroom and gave Anders and Erik a room nearby. Then she led Kate up another flight of stairs to a small room.

"It's the tower!" Kate exclaimed. She felt sure that she stood inside the turret she had seen from outside.

"This was my daughter's room," Mrs. Barclay said softly. "She always said she felt like a princess living here."

In the round outer wall, windows faced in three directions, overlooking Lake Superior. "See the lights of the city?" Mrs. Barclay asked. "You can watch them come on every night."

She pointed to the dark outline of a large building. "That's the Lyceum Theater."

But Kate was already looking beyond the buildings to the

harbor. "I can't believe I'm seeing all this!" she exclaimed.

For the first time since Grandma's disappearance, Kate felt excited about her visit to Duluth. In the growing dusk she spotted the outline of a tall bridge.

"That's our aerial bridge," Mrs. Barclay told her. "It spans the canal between Lake Superior and the bay. There's only one other bridge like it in the world. It's in France."

Two powerful lights shone from the harbor. "Am I seeing two lighthouses?" Kate asked.

"There are two kinds of lighthouses," Mrs. Barclay answered. "The one at the end of the south pier is called an outer or lower range light. A keeper stays there all night to help sailors find their way into the harbor."

"And the other light?" Kate leaned forward for a better look. "The one next to the bridge, I mean."

"It's a tower—a special kind of lighthouse. It's called an inner or upper range light. When a sailor is out at sea, he needs both lights. If he lines one up with the other, he's on course. He heads straight for where he needs to go."

"What if one of the range lights goes out?"

"It happened on Lake Erie a long time ago. Near Cleveland there was a stone breakwater."

"A breakwater?" Kate asked.

"A great pile of stones—a wall built in a long line to protect a harbor from the waves. On a stormy night a steamer tried to reach port. The captain came in at the wrong place, missed the entrance, and crashed into the breakwater."

"There was a shipwreck?" Kate asked.

"The boat smashed to pieces right at the entrance to the harbor. Many lives were lost. A man named Philip Bliss wrote a hymn about the shipwreck. That's what sailors mean when they sing, 'Let the lower lights be burning.' Do you know it?"

Kate shook her head. Just then her stomach growled. Mrs. Barclay smiled. "I'll give you a chance to wash up," she said. "Then come down, and I'll have supper ready."

For the first time since meeting Grandpa, Kate thought of the food Mama had packed. "We have a basket somewhere," she offered. "Anders will eat you out of house and home."

Mrs. Barclay didn't seem too disturbed. "It'll be good to have some healthy boys around for a while."

As Kate settled in for the night, she understood why Mrs. Barclay's daughter wanted this room. She, too, felt like a princess, having her own tower for looking across the city.

During the night it rained. Kate woke to a clap of thunder rattling the house. Lightning streaked across the sky.

Kate crawled out of bed and knelt down next to a window. Clouds blotted out the stars and moon. Except when lightning flashed, blackness hid the water. Yet two bright lights pierced the darkness.

For several minutes Kate watched the harbor. Then she thought about Grandma. It took a long time for Kate to go back to sleep.

————

When Kate entered the kitchen the next morning, Grandpa was already there. Anders and Erik slid into chairs on either side of Kate.

Grandpa bowed his head to give thanks for the meal. But Kate knew his words went far beyond a blessing for the food. She understood a few words. "Our Father in Heaven. Help. Emma." Next she heard her brother's name and Erik's. Then hers. It gave Kate a strange feeling. She had grown used to hearing Mama and Papa Nordstrom pray. Here was another generation, Mama's father, doing the same thing.

Mrs. Barclay brought them ham and eggs and newly baked bread. When they finished eating, Kate and the boys stood up to leave.

"I want to go with you," Grandpa said. He pulled himself up, then wavered on his feet.

Anders shook his head. "Let *us* look," he said. The kindness in his voice surprised Kate. "We might have to walk a long way." Then Anders remembered to speak Swedish for Grandpa.

"Yah! Always I have walked miles at a time!" Grandpa

sounded impatient with his weak knee. "Now when I need my legs most, I cannot!"

Erik rested his hand on the old man's shoulder. He was shorter than either of the boys, and Erik also spoke to him in Swedish. Finally Grandpa nodded, as though sure they would do their best to find his Emma.

As Kate pulled on a coat, Grandpa reached into his pockets, searching for money. When he came up with just a few coins, he shook his head. "All the gold pieces gone! But Grandma is my treasure, my stolen treasure!"

As Kate watched, Grandpa put the coins into her brother's hands.

"*Tack*," Anders said. "It will be enough, enough for the trolley if we need it."

"You rest today," Kate said, and Erik translated. "You get strong."

"Yah," Grandpa answered. "My Emma is the one who is strong." Sudden doubt clouded his eyes. "At least she was the last time I saw her."

As Erik opened the door, Mrs. Barclay gave them a bag of sandwiches. "Superior Street runs east and west through the city," she explained. "Lake Avenue is the dividing line for streets numbering east and west."

"She thinks we'll get lost," Anders muttered as the three left the house.

"Well, maybe we could!" Kate said. "It wouldn't be hard."

They set off for the center of the business district. The steep hill made it easy going down. Each street was lower than the one before.

As they walked, Kate studied the tall houses built on levels carved into the hillside. Between buildings, the roofs were often no more than a foot or two apart.

They found Officer Holmquist outside Union Depot. "I was just going to find you," he said. "Here's the driver you're looking for."

Tony stood beside his team of bays. The big draft horses were hitched to a two-seater buggy. "It's your grandma that's missing, young lady?"

Kate nodded and held out Grandpa's carving. "Her white hair waves back at the sides of her face."

"Yup! I know who you mean. Wore a fur coat. Even with the cold air we get off the lake, it seemed strange this time of year." Tony's smile flashed. "But then—" He shrugged, as though thinking a lot of people do strange things.

"Who was with her?" Kate asked.

"Tall gent. Awful clothes—just awful. Black bowler hat, bent out of shape. Checked suit."

"Checked?"

"Looked like a checkerboard. Navy blue and green. Rumpled up, like he slept in it." Tony's eyes grew hard, as though he didn't like the man.

"Tony took them up the hill," Sergeant Holmquist explained.

"Hop in," the hack driver told them. "I'll drive you up there."

Anders stepped back. "We don't have enough money to pay you."

"I'm going along," the police officer said. "I want to take a look myself. Maybe we'll find something."

As they drove up the hill, Tony told them more. "When the lady got in the buggy, she leaned forward and talked to me. I didn't understand. Is she Swedish or Norwegian?"

"Swedish," Kate said.

"The gent broke in and told me where to go. A few minutes later, I heard him say something to her, soft like. But his voice sounded sharp, kind of hard. I kept my ears perked. The man said, 'Do you want me to take care of your husband?' "

"You could take that two ways." Anders looked worried. "What did he mean?"

"At first I thought it meant he'd take *good* care of her husband," Tony said. "It wasn't until later, after they were gone, that I decided the man could mean just the opposite."

From the front seat Sergeant Holmquist looked back at Anders. "How much English does your grandmother understand?"

"Someone on the ship gave classes," Anders said. "Grandpa told me she was learning all the way over. She kept practicing because she wanted to talk to Kate."

Kate swallowed hard. *But will I ever talk to her?* The more she learned about her grandmother, the more she liked her.

"So maybe your grandma understands what's going on," the sergeant answered.

Anders nodded. "Grandpa said she understood more English than he did. But she couldn't say much."

"When your grandma didn't talk for a while, I looked back," Tony went on. "The fellow smiled at me. Kind of a big grin, full of teeth. The lady looked scared. That's what made me wonder about them. Then the man asked, 'Can you go any faster? She's tired from a long trip.' He seemed to be taking care of her. 'Can't go any faster on this hill,' I told him."

Kate understood why. The street seemed to rise straight up beneath them. The horses leaned into the harness, straining for the hard pull.

As they traveled up the hill, Kate looked left. A block away she saw a high trestle—a framework that held tracks far above the ground. The car that moved along the tracks looked somewhat like a trolley.

Sergeant Holmquist caught her straining to see. "That's the Incline Railway," he said. "People who live in the Heights— Duluth Heights—use the Incline to get up this hill."

Kate could understand why. It would be a difficult climb.

"The Incline rises about 500 feet above Superior Street," Tony told them. "That's the street one block above Union Depot."

Kate nodded. Mrs. Barclay had explained that Superior Street ran parallel to Lake Superior. Businesses and tall buildings lined its two sides.

At the next cross street Kate caught another glimpse of the Incline. "How does it work?"

"Cables. When the conductor wants to move, he calls on a phone to an engineer at the top. Says, 'West car clear!' Or 'East car clear!' Up until the fire there were two cars, one going up, the other down."

"What fire?"

"At the Pavilion. Great big building at the top of the Incline. The fire leveled the Pavilion and spread out of control."

Tony shook his head. "Pretty soon the powerhouse for the Incline caught fire. Right now there's only one car running. But the company will get the other one going again."

The big draft horses took them up the hill to a road that skirted the hillside. As the driver turned onto Boulevard Drive, the buggy leveled out.

Looking back in the direction from which they came, Kate gasped. In the clear morning air, Lake Superior stretched away to the horizon. *Is that the way an ocean looks?* Kate wondered.

From here she could see the high aerial bridge and the canal connecting Lake Superior with the bay. Beyond the canal lay a long peninsula.

"Minnesota Point," Tony said, waving his hand in that direction. "That's the city of Superior off in the distance. See it there on the other side of the bay?" The hills of Wisconsin curved around the bottom of the lake, then disappeared.

A moment later Kate forgot even the view of the harbor. Tony turned his horses onto a level road, then flicked the reins to hurry them. Soon they turned once more, and yet again. By the time the driver stopped the buggy, Kate had lost her sense of direction.

"Right here," he said. "This is where I let your grandma off. Usually I see that people get inside. But the fellow paid me and said, 'Thanks, you don't have to help us.' He and the lady started for the house. I knew he expected me to leave, so I did."

While Tony held the horses, the rest of them climbed down. Sergeant Holmquist led them to the door of the house.

A young woman with a child in her arms answered his knock. A small boy stood near his mother.

"We're looking for an older woman," Sergeant Holmquist said.

To each question he asked, the young woman shook her head. "No one like that has been here."

"Thanks, ma'am," the officer finally said. He walked back to the buggy. "You're sure this is the house?"

Tony nodded, his square jaw set. "I'm sure."

Sergeant Holmquist tried the houses up and down the block

and on both sides of the street. Each time Kate showed the wooden carving of Grandma. No one had seen a woman of her description.

Finally they returned to the buggy. "Let's split up," the policeman said. "See if we can find anything suspicious."

Tony agreed to drive on, looking around, then circle back to pick them up. Anders took another direction, the policeman a third. Kate and Erik stayed together, going off in the fourth direction.

They had walked for a couple of blocks when Kate suddenly stopped. What seemed to be a vacant lot stretched away from the street. Weeds and long grass gave the area an unlived-in look. Yet at the back of the lot, partly hidden by big trees, Kate saw a shack.

Without speaking, she pointed. Erik nodded. Together they struck out across the lot. When they reached the trees, Erik slipped behind a large oak. Kate chose another oak next to his, and they waited, listening.

Smaller trees grew between them and the shack. When no sign of life appeared, Erik started forward. Step by step he and Kate crept to the nearest window.

Erik was tall enough to see inside. He turned away, looking disappointed. "It's empty!"

"You're sure?"

Erik nodded. Just the same, they circled the house. Next to the door, the grass was worn away and the dirt soft from the recent rain.

"Boot prints!" Kate whispered.

Some were blurred, as though they had been there for a time. Yet there were also sharp, fresh prints, as if recently made.

Kate stared at the prints. "Two people were here! I'm sure of it!"

7

The Incline Railway

$\mathscr{A}$t one side of the dirt Kate saw the wide rounded toe of a large boot. The heel sank deep into the ground, as if the man were tall or heavy.

Nearby, a much smaller set of prints seemed to be made by a woman's shoes. At the center of the softest dirt the toes faced out, away from the shack.

"Strange!" Kate felt troubled. "It looks like she purposely made the clearest prints she could."

"As if she wanted to tell us she was leaving. You know, Kate, if those are your grandma's footprints, she's pretty smart!"

"Smart and worried. Do you think she's trying to leave a trail?"

"Well, I bet she's not in the house." Erik sounded grim. He took only a moment to peer through another window. From this side, too, the house seemed to be deserted.

"Let's get Sergeant Holmquist," he said.

The others were waiting when Kate and Erik returned to the spot where they agreed to meet. No one else had found anything. While Tony stayed with his horses, Anders and the policeman followed Kate and Erik back to the shack.

When they tried the door, they found it unlocked. It swung open on creaking hinges. Kate and Erik and Anders followed Officer Holmquist inside.

The room they entered was small with only the two windows through which Erik had looked. The boards that made up the outside walls were rough and dirty on the inside. Water stains showed on the ceiling, leaving brown marks where the roof leaked. The floor was nothing more than firmly packed dirt.

Opposite the door, a wide shelf was nailed to the wooden supports of the wall. Waist high, the shelf held the only object in the room—a rusty old basin.

A narrow doorway led off the main room into an even smaller one. Kate could barely see through the dirt clouding the only window. A chair with a broken back leaned against the wall.

In spite of herself, Kate shivered. Where had Grandma sat— on the dirt floor or the only chair? Kate was afraid that she knew the answer. Grandma and the man might have come here right after leaving the depot. *Two nights ago*, Kate thought. *Did Grandma wait two long nights and one day in this shack?* There was no way of knowing.

Even worse, there was no stove in the building, no heat against the cool night air. Again, Kate shivered, but her trembling had nothing to do with the temperature.

She looked carefully around, then walked back into the main room. She had hoped Grandma would leave something that told them the woman's footprints belonged to her.

As Kate watched, Sergeant Holmquist started at the wall next to the door and worked his way around the room, searching. Anders and Erik did the same in the smaller room. With the dim light it was hard to see anything but dirt.

Kate swung the door wide open. As she turned back, sunlight streamed through the doorway, striking the basin. The shelf on which it sat was slightly crooked, yet the basin tipped even more.

Why? Kate wondered. She walked over to the shelf and picked up the basin.

Underneath lay a small knitted square, just big enough to give a slight tip to the basin. The square was fresh and clean, as if newly knitted. Most important of all, the yarn was red.

Kate called to the others. "Look what I found!"

"Did Grandpa say that Grandma was knitting red mittens?" Anders asked.

Kate nodded. She felt good about her discovery.

Erik grinned. "Grandma was here, all right!"

Yet his eyes looked worried. Seeing them, Kate felt awful.

"I don't understand," the sergeant said.

Kate explained about the gift of red yarn. "Grandpa says Grandma knitted mittens all the way across the ocean. If she put a mitten under the basin, the man would have seen it. That's probably why she knitted this small piece. She must have carried the yarn and needles in her bag."

Kate gave Sergeant Holmquist the red square.

"I'll keep it for evidence," he said. "Let's finish searching, then follow their trail."

Within a few minutes they covered every inch of the shack. No one found anything more.

When they went back outside, the sergeant measured the prints in the dirt. He wrote down their size in a notebook.

"How old are the prints?" Kate asked.

The sergeant looked Kate in the eye. "Can't say for sure, but they seem very recent."

"Do you think she was here for two nights? Two nights and a day?" Kate dreaded the thought.

"Maybe," the sergeant said, as though trying to offer comfort and honesty at the same time.

Kate moved off the wooden step into the sunlight. After only a short time in the dirty shack, she wanted to be far from it. She wondered how her grandmother could have stood it.

Around the house, weeds and grass grew high. "Let's spread out again," the sergeant said. "Be careful that you don't step on anything that would help us."

Each of them headed for a different corner of the yard. This time it was Erik who found something—a pressed-down line of grass leading off into a thick growth of trees.

"Deer?" Erik asked.

Since moving to northwest Wisconsin, Kate had never seen one of them. Though once plentiful, whitetail deer had become scarce in that area.

The sergeant nodded. "They probably come here to graze. No one around to bother them—most of the time, that is!"

Erik led them a short distance into the trail. On one side of the faint path the brown leaves of winter were kicked aside. In the center of a patch of dirt was the print of a woman's shoe.

"It's the same as before!" Kate exclaimed.

Setting off through the woods, they followed the deer path, looking for more boot prints. The longer they hiked, the more nervous Kate felt. Grandma was more than twenty years older than Mama. How much physical activity could the older woman take?

They had walked several blocks when they came to a trampled down area of grass. Next to the grass, a thick line of bushes bordered a road.

"Bet that old crook stood here," Anders muttered. "Made sure no one else was around when he came out on the road."

Sergeant Holmquist and the boys passed through a narrow opening between the bushes. As they entered a dirt road, the policeman looked one direction, then the other. Which way had the man taken Grandma?

Kate was last to slip between the bushes. At one side of the opening, a branch reached out, snagging the yarn in her coat. Working carefully, she freed the yarn without breaking the thread.

"Hurry up, Kate!" Anders called.

As she lifted the last thread, Kate noticed the bush on the other side of the opening. At the end of two branches, small twigs were bent back. Kate called the others.

"Did any of you break some twigs?"

Anders stared blankly at her. Erik shook his head. The sergeant came back.

"See the twigs on the end of these branches?" she said. "They're broken, but not off. Broken just enough to turn the ends. All the ends point in the same direction!"

The sergeant grinned. "I'm starting to get a real good feeling about your grandmother. She's got a lot of old-fashioned spunk!"

Following the direction of the bent twigs, they took a right turn on the road. Though searching on both sides, they walked fast. Always they watched for a place where the man could have led Grandma off the road.

Soon the woods fell away, and they followed the sergeant into an area of houses. For some time they continued to search. Finally they were forced to admit they had reached a dead end.

"I'm going back to the station for more men," Sergeant Holmquist said. "Want to come along?"

Kate shook her head. Though they had searched for some time, leaving the area seemed to be leaving Grandma behind.

"If you need help, our station is at 126 East Superior Street. It's a brownstone building with our name over the door."

The sergeant set off in the direction of Tony and the hack. Kate sank onto the ground, and the boys dropped down beside her.

By now the sun was high in the sky. Here, at the top of the hill, it was growing warm. Kate pulled off her coat and tied it around her waist. As she pushed back the wisps of hair escaping her braid, she longed for the cooler air close to the lake.

"Kate, would your grandma recognize you if she saw you?" Erik asked.

Kate thought about it. "Maybe," she answered. "When we lived in Minneapolis, Mama sent her a picture of me. But that was over two years ago—before Daddy O'Connell died. I've changed a lot since then."

"Well, there's one thing in our favor," Erik said. "Grandma is doing everything she can to leave a trail."

Kate felt proud of her grandmother. "And she's leaving that trail without being able to write English!"

"You know what else?" For the first time that morning Erik did not look worried. "Grandma reminds me of you, Kate."

"Of me?" Kate was startled.

"Of the way you act."

"Yah, sure," Anders blurted out. "The way Kate manages to

find trouble. She always gets herself into something strange and different."

"That's not what I mean," Erik said to Kate. "Your grandma's doing everything she can to win."

Kate caught the sideways compliment. She blinked under Erik's steady gaze. She almost felt scared—scared and full of something she couldn't explain.

When she smiled at Erik, he seemed to understand. But Anders broke in again.

"That Kate, she wants to win all right."

Kate ignored him and spoke to Erik. "Even though I'm proud of Grandma, what she's doing bothers me. Grandma wouldn't leave a trail unless she knew she was in danger."

Erik stood up, as though he'd already thought of the same thing. Kate and Anders stood too, and all three of them went back to their search. Each one chose a larger area than they had examined before.

When they came together again, Anders looked excited. "C'mon! I'll show you. I left it just the way I found it."

After walking some distance, Anders stopped next to a tall bush that grew over the road. Beneath its spreading branches, there was soft dirt. Kate saw what they had found twice before—the print of a woman's shoe!

It was close to the road, as if whoever made it swung to the right for two or three steps. Beyond the print, Kate saw something red, mostly covered with dirt.

She got down on her hands and knees. Without disturbing the shoe print, she pushed aside the nearby dirt and uncovered a red mitten! It looked as though someone had dropped the mitten, then stepped on it, pushing it partway into the ground. Soft earth had fallen over the sides, but the middle of the mitten remained free to be seen.

Kate took a small stick and drew an outline around the mitten. Then she picked it up and shook off the dirt. "It hasn't been here long," she said as the soil fell away.

Carefully Kate turned the mitten over. She had done enough knitting to know that it was skillfully made. The workmanship told her something else about her grandmother.

Kate bit her lip. Even holding something the older woman had knitted increased Kate's longing to know her.

"Let's keep looking," Erik said.

"But where?" For the second time in less than twenty-four hours, Kate felt angry. Angry at the conductor who failed to tell Grandpa and Grandma to get off the train at Rush City. Angry at the man who had stolen Grandma away. Angry about all the difficulties and disappointments in finding her.

Without answering, Anders climbed onto a large rock and looked in every direction.

"We're back close to the Incline Railway." He pointed to an opening between houses.

As Kate looked that way, she saw the trestle high above the ground. They had circled around so much she had become confused in her directions.

As Anders dropped down off the rock, Kate looked once more under the bush. For the first time she realized something.

"The footprint is pointing toward the Incline!"

Anders grinned. "You betcha! Let's go!"

8

Central High Search

$\mathcal{T}$he three broke into a run. At last it felt as if they were doing something. By the time they reached the Incline Railway, Kate's side ached.

Steps led up to the high trestle and a platform. As they climbed the stairs, Kate paused to catch her breath. "How do we know?" she asked when she could speak again. "How can we be sure Grandma took the Incline?"

"We don't know," her brother said. "It's one long guess. But what else can we do?"

The stairs brought them to a waiting room built between two sets of tracks. When the cable car arrived, Kate was the first one through its side doorway.

A conductor waited there to collect fares. Anders dug deep into a pocket and came up with a nickel for each of them. The conductor handed them pieces of paper for transferring onto a trolley.

Kate hurried forward to the downhill side of the car. Though hugging a very steep hill, the floor of the cable car was level. Kate slipped into an empty seat next to the front window.

Once again she found a breathtaking view of Lake Superior

and the bay. Along the southern rim, the hills of Wisconsin disappeared in a blue haze.

Tall smokestacks lined the shore of the bay between Duluth and Superior. Sawmills, Kate decided. A long train, loaded high with logs, snaked its way toward one of the sheds.

Farther away, great trestles reached out into the bay. Along the tracks, railroad cars transferred their shipment of ore to large freighters.

"Look at the grain elevators!" Erik exclaimed when he and Anders joined Kate.

The great buildings stood close to the water. Even at this distance, Kate saw a huge ship tied alongside, receiving its cargo of grain.

The aerial bridge spanning the canal between Lake Superior and the bay stood sharply outlined against the water. Beyond, a long road led between the houses on Minnesota Point.

"On a clear day you can see forty miles up the lake," Kate heard the conductor say. As she turned around, he closed the door, then spoke into a telephone. "West car clear!"

A moment later the cable car eased forward, beginning its slow trip down the hill. At the side of the track Kate saw large houses similar to the one in which Mrs. Barclay lived.

Within a few blocks, the car creaked to a stop to take on passengers. Twice more the car stopped. The tall buildings of Duluth's business district drew close.

At the stop between First and Second Street, Kate and the boys left the car. When they came out on the platform, they looked down the hill to Superior Street. A trolley rumbled across the intersection.

Kate headed for the stairs leading from the platform. With one bound she reached the ground. "What should we try next?" she asked as they hurried down the rest of the hill.

"If Grandma and that crook were on the Incline, they'd get a transfer just like us," Erik said.

On Superior Street they came to a cluster of people waiting for the next trolley. Kate walked around them, searching the sidewalk for a red mitten or a piece of yarn.

Anders and Erik started asking questions. Outside a nearby building a man was washing windows. "Yup, I saw a woman that looks like that," he said. "She was wearing a fur coat."

He looked up at the sun beating down upon him. Though his shirt sleeves were rolled up, there were beads of sweat on his forehead. "Seemed mighty strange on a warm day like this."

"Did you notice where she went?" Anders asked.

"She left the man she was with, walking mighty fast. When she started across the street, an automobile came along. She couldn't run out in front of it."

The window washer wiped the sweat off his forehead. "The man caught up and grabbed her arm. Told her, 'You're going the wrong way.' His eyes looked mean."

"Mean?" asked Kate, her voice little more than a whisper. Was this the same man who had been at the depot asking questions? *Like he was holding a grudge, the hack driver said. But why would someone have a grudge against Grandma?*

"Mean," the window washer repeated. "I thought he was mad at the way the lady acted. She seemed confused. They took the trolley going east."

"How long ago?" Anders asked.

"Not more than ten minutes—maybe less."

"Ten minutes?" Kate's stomach tightened with disappointment. They had just missed Grandma. What could they do to catch up?

As they waited for the next trolley, Kate paced up and down the sidewalk. Finally she stopped in front of the boys. "I don't understand what's going on," she said. "When Grandma is with people, why doesn't she make a great big fuss to get help?"

"What makes you think she doesn't?" Erik asked. "Look at how she tried to talk to Tony. And that other hack driver didn't realize she was held against her will until it was too late."

"The window washer said she walked away," Anders said. "All the man has to do is hold her elbow. People think he's helping an older woman."

Kate's uneasy stomach churned. "So it looks as if he's helping her walk?"

Her brother nodded. "I'm afraid so. We're going to have to hunt mighty hard to figure out where they got off the trolley."

"Well, there's one thing." Kate tried to push her worry aside. "Grandma has lots of mittens to drop. Grandpa said she knitted the whole way across the Atlantic."

It seemed forever before another trolley came along. Brakes squealing, it rolled to a stop.

Inside, the conductor took their transfers. Kate and Erik dropped down on a seat opposite the doorway. Anders took a seat across the aisle so he could watch the other side of the street.

"You really care about Grandma, don't you?" Kate asked Erik as they waited for the rest of the passengers to get on.

"All four of my grandparents live in Sweden," he answered. "I'll never get to meet them."

"That's how I used to feel. Maybe someday you'll see your grandparents—the way I've met Grandpa."

Erik shook his head. "I don't think so. My grandparents don't have the money to come to America, and we don't have the money to help them."

He looked away, avoiding Kate's eyes, as if he didn't want her to see how much it bothered him.

No, you'll meet them someday, Kate wanted to say. Then she knew she couldn't. Instead, she had to admit to herself, *Maybe Erik is right. Maybe he never will see his grandparents.* It was very unusual for people to come a long distance for a visit.

Through Kate's mind flashed the faces of her friends at Spirit Lake School and friends living in Minneapolis. Some of them had grandparents in America. But many had immigrant parents like hers—immigrants who left everyone behind in order to come here. How many of her friends were like Erik—never to see their grandparents because they lived far across the ocean?

Then Erik looked back at Kate. As though he had just made a decision, he said, "Someday I'll earn enough money to help my grandparents come over."

"Good idea." Kate's voice was soft. "Till then, my grandparents can be *your* grandparents."

Erik grinned. "Then we better find my new grandma right away!"

When the conductor released the brake, the trolley eased forward, then picked up speed. Kate stared out the window, hoping somehow to spot a new clue.

Tall buildings rose from either side of the street. When the trolley stopped near Fifth Avenue West, Kate saw a large building on her left.

"Brownstone," Erik said. "Mrs. Barclay told me about the quarries around here."

Beneath a great archway, several steps led to the entryway. "There above the door—see its name?" asked Erik. "The Lyceum."

"That's the theater she talked about last night." Kate craned her neck and saw stone masks on either side of the arch. "One's a happy face. The other, sad."

She turned back to Erik. "That's how I feel right now. One part of me is really sad. But if I knew Grandma was all right, it would be fun to see all of this."

A block later the trolley turned and started up Third Avenue. It strained ahead on the steep hill.

All Kate could think about was the long arm going up to the wire overhead. *What if the electricity goes out? What if we roll backward?* She leaned forward as if she could help the trolley up the bluff.

Four blocks farther on, the trolley turned again onto Second Street. As it leveled out and rumbled east, Kate felt relieved.

"I wish I had ten eyes," she muttered as she tried to see everything. Most of all, she wanted to see Grandma.

As the trolley stopped once more, Kate gazed ahead and forgot everything else. "Look at *that!*"

A curved stairway led up the hill to a brownstone building that covered most of the block. At the center of the building a tall clock tower pointed to the sky. Kate searched for a name and found it over the entrance: CENTRAL HIGH SCHOOL.

"A *school?*" Kate asked Erik. She felt unable to tear her gaze from the building. "*That's* a school?"

She couldn't help but think of the log school she attended at home. All eight grades—58 students—met in one room. What would it be like to attend a school such as Central? Kate couldn't even imagine it.

As the trolley rolled past the main entrance, Kate saw a second set of stairs curving up to meet the first. On the third step from the bottom lay a red mitten.

Kate jumped up. "C'mon!" She ran to the trolley door and pounded on it.

"Just pull the cord, little lady," the conductor called. "I'll stop at any block you want."

A flush of embarrassment warmed Kate's cheeks. Already she'd forgotten all she knew from riding streetcars in Minneapolis.

"What's wrong?" Erik asked as he and Anders followed Kate to the ground.

As soon as the trolley passed them, Kate crossed the street. "I'll show you," she said. She hurried back to Central High School.

When she reached the steps, she pounced on the mitten. "But why would the stranger take Grandma *here*?"

"He must know someone would try to follow him." Erik's voice sounded thoughtful. "I bet he's trying to lose whoever it might be."

Anders looked up at the huge building. "Well, this sure looks like a good place for doing that."

Kate continued up the stairs. Far above, in raised letters cut from stone, she saw the name of the school again. Before her were still more steps, then a large entryway.

When she passed through the center doors, she found herself in a hallway that ran the length of the building. Just looking at the many doors, Kate felt confused. With the great number of rooms, where could her grandmother be?

"Well, Grandma won't be in a classroom," Anders muttered as though hearing Kate's thoughts. "That man can't take Grandma where a teacher would see him."

"Let's split up again," Erik said. "Meet here at the front entrance as soon as possible."

As Kate set off down the wide hallway, classes let out. A

stream of students hurrying to their next class surrounded her.

Kate fell into step behind a girl wearing a white high-necked blouse and a black skirt. As the girl passed a doorway, a boy hurried out of a classroom and bumped into her.

"Sorry!" the boy exclaimed.

"That's all right!"

As the girl continued down the hallway, Kate spotted a large bow lying on the floor.

"Wait a minute!" Kate called, but the girl didn't seem to hear. Kate hurried after her with the hair ribbon.

"Oh, thanks!" the girl said as Kate gave it to her. "I'm glad I didn't lose it."

She took a better look at Kate. "I haven't seen you before. Are you a new student?"

A high school student? Inside, Kate glowed. She knew she didn't look that old, but it felt good to be asked.

"I'm not a student," Kate said and learned the girl's name was Betsy. "I'm looking for my grandmother. Have you seen anyone that looks like a grandmother walking around?"

Betsy stared at Kate. "It's kind of an odd place for a grandma to be, isn't it? Especially when you aren't a student here."

Kate explained quickly. Betsy's expression changed to concern.

"I know it's a strange question," Kate said finally. "But if that man brought her here, where could he hide her?"

Betsy thought for a moment. "The clock tower! That would be a perfect hiding place! Students aren't allowed to go there— most of the time, that is."

Kate remembered the enormous tower she had seen from outside. "But how could someone get up there?"

Betsy laughed. "It's easy! Of all the students in the school, you came to the right person. I'll show you."

9

Narrow Escape!

*B*etsy took Kate up a stairway to the third floor. "Usually the tower is locked," she explained. "But I'm on the stage crew, and we store scenery here. We've been setting up for a play the seniors give at the end of the year."

Betsy winked. "That's how I manage to get out of classes now and then."

Kate followed her into a large square room. Betsy pointed to a trapdoor in the center of the ceiling. "When we aren't using the scenery, we lift it through that hole to the floors above."

She led Kate up a flight of open stairs. Each tread was made of a wide board. With every step Kate took, she looked between the boards to the floor far below. The higher she went, the more nervous she felt. If she fell, it was a long way down!

Betsy seemed unconcerned about the dangers of the tower. The next level seemed much like the first. Kate looked around for any sign of Grandma. Instead, she once again noticed the large trapdoor for lifting scenery to the floors above.

Another stairway led upward. "How do you like all the names on the walls?" Betsy asked.

Kate saw the inside brick of the tower was covered with writing.

"Just before graduation, teachers bring the seniors here, class by class. They write their names and the year they graduate. I'm not a senior, but I wrote mine."

Betsy pointed. "Nice and big. I put it there yesterday when I was working."

Halfway up the flight of steps, Kate slowed down. A thought real enough to be a voice warned her. *Grandma isn't here. You're wasting time.*

Kate called to Betsy. "Let's go back. It's too many steps for an older person."

"Oh, Kate, are you *sure*? You won't get to stand inside the clock."

"This is the wrong place."

Betsy moaned. "You won't get to stand inside the clock. Or look out the top of the tower. Or see the hammers strike the four bells."

But Kate had already turned around. She hurried down the steps as fast as she dared go. "Time could mean my grandma's life! Where else could someone hide?"

When they reached the bottom of the tower, Betsy had an idea. "Let's try the auditorium—the large room where we give plays. If no one is working there, it'd be a good hideout."

She set off, walking fast. "I'll show you the quickest way there."

Once she turned and said, "I wish you lived here so we could be friends."

Kate's heart warmed to Betsy's friendliness. But when they reached the auditorium, Kate warned her, "We have to be careful. If we find that man, we can't let him see us."

Betsy opened the door without making a sound and slipped inside.

As Kate followed, she looked up to a curved balcony around the three outer walls of the room. Far above, draperies decorated the arched windows. The heavy curtains seemed to be made of velvet. The same kind of curtains closed off the stage.

When Betsy began to speak, Kate whispered, "Shhhh!" She pointed toward the stage.

"The floor squeaks," Betsy whispered back. "Follow me."

Avoiding certain boards, she led Kate toward the curtains. As they drew close, Kate heard a low murmur on the other side.

"Stop it!" The man's voice sounded sharp. "I know my way around this school."

The answer came in Swedish. Kate understood a few of the words. "Foolish. Peter." Something about "finding." She caught only one complete sentence. "I am not who you think I am."

"Whether you like it or not, I'll tell you again," the man replied. He spoke slowly, as though talking to a child. "I . . . know . . . who . . . you . . . are."

Mean, Kate thought. *He's mean, all right.* Fear squeezed her heart. *Who does he think Grandma is?*

"Now listen to me," the man said. "If you make a big fuss, I'll hurt your husband."

Kate backed away from the stage. Again Betsy led her across the floor. They had almost reached the door when Kate stepped on the wrong board.

The floor creaked loudly. Kate glanced toward the curtain and saw a large hand push it aside. Then Betsy flung open the door, and they both slipped through.

Kate fled through the hallway. Betsy's footsteps sounded loud on the marble floor.

"Do you think he saw us?" she asked as they turned a corner.

"I'm afraid so!" Kate ran as she'd never run before.

When they reached the place where Kate was to meet Anders and Erik, the boys weren't there. Kate felt frantic. *What can I do to get help?*

Then she remembered the school office she had seen. Betsy pointed her in the right direction.

A teacher, a man with gray hair, stopped them. "No running in the halls!"

"Please!" Kate gasped. She stopped, caught her breath. "I need help!" Her words tumbled out so fast that the teacher couldn't understand.

Kate stopped, caught her breath, and started over. This time she spoke more slowly.

In spite of the strangeness of her story, the teacher finally nodded. "Let's go to the office. I'll get help."

Once there, he hurried past a secretary into an inner room. From where she stood, Kate heard people talking. Soon the teacher returned, with two men following him.

"We'll go with you," one of them said. Kate wondered if he was the principal.

The teacher headed down the hall. As Kate followed, she saw Anders and Erik. "C'mon!" she motioned.

When they reached the auditorium, the teacher stopped.

"If you're quiet when you go in, you'll hear the man talking," Kate said. "He's on the stage."

The teacher opened the door. The three men, Kate and Betsy, Erik and Anders walked toward the heavy curtains.

For a minute they stood there, listening. Finally the teacher looked at Kate. "It was here you heard someone?"

Kate nodded. "Right here." But no sound came from the stage.

The teacher walked forward. As though wondering if Kate were trying to make a fool of him, he pushed back the curtain. On the other side, the stage was empty!

Looking stern, the principal turned to Kate. "It's a serious offense to pretend there's something wrong when there isn't."

"I know," Kate answered, feeling embarrassed. "I'm sorry, sir. But my grandma is missing, and I heard her talking. The man probably saw us when we left. Somehow he got away."

Just then a door slammed. The sound echoed in the large room.

Anders raced across to the other end of the auditorium. In the corner farthest from the stage they found a metal door. NO ADMITTANCE, the large letters said.

"That door is always locked!" the teacher exclaimed as he and the others caught up.

"If Kate is right, locks don't make any difference," the principal said. "The man knows how to open them."

He pulled out a set of keys and found the right one. The door opened to an empty passageway. "You're sure you heard someone talking?" he asked Kate.

She nodded. "I'm sure."

"I heard him too," Betsy said. "And I heard a woman."

The principal turned around. "Betsy, you go back to class."

Betsy moaned, as though wishing she had stayed quiet. She looked disappointed, but the principal looked stern.

"Bye, Kate," Betsy said. "I hope you find your grandma." She reached back, pulled the bow from her hair, and gave it to Kate. "Friends for life!" she said dramatically.

"Thanks, Betsy," Kate said. "Thanks for everything!" Quickly she fastened the bow at the top of her braid.

The principal led them through a passageway into the furnace room. Huge boilers filled the space. Kate circled them, looking for Grandma.

On the far side of the room, a door stood partly open. Kate hurried over. Beyond, she found a carriage house and another open door.

"My horses!" exclaimed a voice behind her. "My horses are gone!"

10

Rooftop Walkway

*K*ate whirled around. She stared at the man who had come with the teacher and principal.

"I put my horses here when I came," he said. "They've always been safe before."

But the carriage house stood empty. No horses. No buggies. No people.

The man told Kate and the boys that his name was Schulz. "Well, I hope the thief doesn't run my horses to death!"

Kate gazed at the empty carriage house as if she couldn't believe yet another setback. But Erik asked, "What do your horses look like?"

"They're a team of matched grays," Mr. Schulz answered. "People know them. The thief will realize he can't take them far without being recognized."

Listening to him, Kate thought of something. It gave her new hope. "If we find your horses, maybe we'll find my grandmother. So how can we find your horses?"

Mr. Schulz considered the question. "The thief might leave them at a livery stable. He could pretend the horses belong to him. He would just ask the stable to take care of them until he comes back."

"He might act as if he has business downtown," the principal said. "That would be less obvious than leaving the horses on a street."

With a quick thanks for their help, Kate, Anders, and Erik left the teacher and principal behind. The Duluth business section was just a short walk down the hill.

As Mr. Schulz led the way, Anders questioned Kate. "If you heard the thief talk to Grandma, did you understand anything they said?"

"Everything *he* said." Kate repeated the man's words.

Anders and Erik exchanged looks. Kate felt pretty sure she knew what they were thinking. She felt the same way—as if she were on a huge wave, being washed out to sea.

"I understood a few of Grandma's words—*Peter* and *find*. She must have been talking about Grandpa. But I caught only one complete sentence, 'I am not who you think I am.' The man answered, 'I know who you are.' "

Two and a half blocks from Central High School they came to the first livery stable. Mr. Schulz walked past the stalls, then questioned the man in charge.

"Nope! No horses like that today!" came the reply.

The second stable was a block beyond that, on Second Avenue West. The attendant shook his head. No team of matched grays had been there.

The third livery was three blocks from the second and the largest stable of all. In the office on First Street Mr. Schulz asked again about his horses.

"Yup! I've got 'em here," the owner said. "Wondered about 'em when they came in. Didn't like the looks of the man driving 'em."

"Who was in the buggy?" Erik asked.

"White-haired lady. Gent wearing a checked suit—blue and green checks, I think it was."

The owner turned back to Mr. Schulz. "Want to see your horses?"

Mr. Schulz looked grim. "I certainly do."

It took only a minute for him to check the grays and see that they were all right.

Kate felt glad for Mr. Schulz and expected him to leave.

Instead, he said, "Well, that tells us where the thief went. But we still don't know the most important thing. What happened to your grandmother?"

Kate felt surprised at his question. A small scared place deep inside felt glad for his kindness.

"Any idea where the people went?" Mr. Schulz asked the owner.

"If they planned ahead, I'd put my money on a hotel room," he said. "The lady looked all wore out."

"There are at least ten hotels in a six- or seven-block area," Mr. Schulz told Kate and the boys.

"Let's try the closest ones first," Erik said, and asked their names.

Mr. Schulz knew where there was a telephone and went to call the police.

"Ask for Sergeant Holmquist," Anders said. "Tell him we followed Grandma down the Incline to Central High School and here. He'll know what to do next."

Kate, Anders, and Erik agreed where to meet. Erik set off for the Hotel McKay, Anders for the Hotel St. Louis, and Kate for the Spalding House Hotel.

On the corner of Fifth Avenue West, Kate stared up at the large hotel. The brownstone building extended along Superior Street and back a block to the next street.

Kate tried to guess at the number of floors. Seven perhaps? With all of those rooms the possibility of finding Grandma seemed hopeless.

As Kate approached the entry, a uniformed man opened the door. Inside, Kate walked across a shining wood floor, then a red rug with big flowers. More flowers decorated large vases that stood on the tables or floor.

Kate found the hotel clerk behind a high counter with a grille much like those in banks. She asked if he had seen someone of Grandma's description.

"I just started working a few minutes ago," the clerk answered, and Kate believed him. At the same time she wondered whether he was allowed to give out information about guests.

As Kate turned away from the desk, she looked once more around the lobby. Beyond the reds and golds, the plush rug and the beautiful wood paneling, there was something she needed to understand. A small nudge, a thought, teased at the back of her mind. What was it?

Then Kate knew. Deep inside, she felt certain about something. If the man they were following could help it, he wouldn't stay in this public a room. Where would he go?

A wide stairway led off the lobby, but Kate saw nothing that drew her there. Were there elevators?

It took only a moment to locate them, and when she did, her heart leaped. In front of the double doors lay a bright red mitten!

Kate snatched it up. *They're only a few steps ahead of me!* People working in such a beautiful hotel wouldn't leave something lying on the floor.

Just then the elevator doors opened. "Going up!" the operator called out. Kate stepped on and asked for the second floor.

Quickly she searched the long corridors for any clue that Grandma had been there. When Kate found nothing, she went on to the third floor, then the fourth.

By now she needed to meet the boys. Kate returned to the first floor and hurried through the lobby to Superior Street. She found Erik and Anders coming from two directions.

As Kate told them about the mitten, they followed her back into the Spalding Hotel. Next to the elevator doors Kate stopped.

"What are you waiting for?" Anders asked.

"The elevator, of course." Kate flipped her long braid over her shoulder.

Her brother asked no more questions, as though unwilling to admit he had never ridden on one. Yet his eyes were alert, watchful.

Soon the doors opened, and the operator called out, "Going up!"

"Fifth floor," Kate said as she entered the elevator.

Ha! she thought gleefully as the boys followed her. In the country they always seemed to know more than she did. Now, having lived in Minneapolis, Kate had the advantage.

As the elevator moved from floor to floor, she reached back and felt the ribbon Betsy had given her. *Maybe I look like a city girl*, Kate thought with satisfaction.

At the fifth floor she stepped off as though she had ridden the elevator every day of her life. On each of the remaining floors, Kate and the boys searched the corridors, looking for another clue.

Finally they came out at the top of the building. There they discovered a covered walkway on the roof.

Standing at the railing, Kate looked down. Sounds carried clearly from the avenue several stories below. Across the street and to Kate's right was the Union Depot. People hurried in and out of its large covered entrance.

Railroad tracks crossed the area directly in front of Kate. Beyond that, and four or five blocks to her left, a street led down to the aerial bridge.

"Look at that big ship going through the canal!" she exclaimed.

"It's called a freighter," Anders said, and Kate wondered if he was trying to prove how much he knew.

Like a magnet, the waterfront drew her. She wanted to be close to everything that was going on. "I wish we could go down there," she said.

"We will," Erik promised. "We'll walk along the canal."

From here it was easy to see the inner and outer range lights on the south pier. Kate told the boys how sailors lined up one light with the other to guide their ships into port.

Then, once again, Kate's concern for her grandmother pushed aside every other thought. "Where *is* she, do you think?"

Erik knew what Kate meant. "I wish we could open every hotel room. That's probably the only way we'll find out."

"We need to talk to the police again," Anders said.

"The police!" Kate exclaimed. "We forgot to tell Sergeant

Holmquist about the mitten. Is there a telephone here?"

"I'll go find out," Anders said. He started toward the elevator.

Again Kate remembered her feeling that the man would not want to stay in this public a place. "I don't think they'll be here long," she said to Erik. "How would that man leave if he didn't want to go through the lobby?"

"There must be a service door on the back side of the hotel." Erik looked around. "That's the side we're on."

Gazing down, he and Kate stared at the building directly below them. They couldn't see if there was a door, but someone was walking on the sidewalk.

The man wore a black bowler hat and a checked suit. He clutched the elbow of the woman walking beside him. The woman had white hair.

"It's Grandma!" Kate cried.

She whirled around. "Anders, come here!"

When her brother didn't respond, Kate raised her voice. "Anders! It's Grandma!"

Once more Kate looked over the railing. As she stared down, the man and woman looked up.

"Kate!" Erik warned. "Stand back! They heard you." Before Kate could think, he pulled her away from the railing.

"They heard?" she asked, her voice small. "From way up here?"

Erik looked grim. "You were yelling, you know."

He leaned over the railing. "Look!" he said.

Kate stared down. Using the man's moment of surprise, Grandma had hurried off down the street. But the man caught up and grabbed her arm again.

"They're getting away!" Kate cried. "We've got to catch them!"

Whirling around, she headed for the elevator. When it didn't come, the three searched for the stairs. Down flight after flight they ran. At last they reached the ground floor.

Through the hotel lobby they raced, searching for a back door. They came out on the street just below the rooftop walkway. The sidewalk was empty.

11

Footsteps in the Fog

$\mathcal{A}$w, Kate!" Anders complained. "How could you do that to us? You and your big mouth!"

Kate clenched her fists, having all she could do not to throttle her brother. He was right, she knew. But something else made matters worse. She had made things even more difficult for Grandma.

Closing her eyes, Kate leaned back against the building and counted to ten. When that didn't help, she counted again. She felt angry at Anders, but even more angry with herself.

"We're in for it now!" Anders grumbled.

Kate's eyes flew open. "What do you mean? It's Grandma who's in for it!"

"So are we. You've managed to tell that guy that we're following them. What's to keep him from coming after *us*?"

Kate drew back. Even the idea of having that awful man follow her seemed scary.

Then Kate tossed her long braid over a shoulder. "Why would he do that?" She straightened to her full height, short as that was.

Even so, Anders towered above her. "Because the crook

knows we could stop his plans for Grandma. He's seen you twice—at the high school and now here."

Kate sagged against the building once more. Again her brother was right. What was worse, she couldn't get her last sight of Grandma out of her mind. The man held Grandma's arm as though making sure she wouldn't get away.

"Let's figure out what to do next," Erik said.

"Yah, Kate," Anders muttered. "What do you want to do now?"

Kate sighed. She looked up and down the block—Michigan Street, it was called. In front of them were tracks and the Northern Pacific freight depot. Farther down the street, the tracks passed close to a loading platform for a wholesale grocer.

"When you first saw the man, which way was he going?" Erik asked.

Kate pointed east.

"Well, since we don't know what else to do, let's try that," Erik suggested.

Erik and Anders set off down the street. Kate followed, but her heart was heavy. Soon they passed more wholesalers—Swift and Company meat, a place selling fruit, others offering paper and poultry.

Farther on, a packing company advertised cold storage. Nowhere was there a clue about Grandma's whereabouts.

Five blocks from the Spalding Hotel they came to Lake Avenue.

"Maybe you get your wish, Kate," Erik said. "This street leads down to Lake Superior. Should we take it?" He turned to Anders.

"You betcha."

The blocks to the canal took them past more businesses and several large boardinghouses. Near a building marked *U.S. Corps of Engineers* was the aerial bridge they had seen from far away.

Two gigantic steel towers reached upward, one on either side of the canal. The towers supported a long span of steel girders that crossed the waterway.

From a track on that span, more girders held a suspended transfer car. Like a ferry, the transfer car moved back and forth between the city of Duluth and the peninsula of Minnesota Point.

As Kate and the boys watched, the car crossed the canal and came to rest over the land near where they stood. Passengers streamed out of two glassed-in cabins. Teams of horses with wagons followed the people off the ferry.

Just then a boat whistled its signal. Kate, Anders, and Erik joined the others who hurried to the pier. As they leaned against the concrete rail at the edge of the walkway, the ship passed from the bay through the canal.

The long, narrow boat rode low in the water. Its steel sides and deck tapered almost to a point in front and back.

At first Kate thought the ship looked like a floating cigar. Then it drew closer. The front of the boat rounded up to meet the upper deck.

Kate giggled. "It looks like a pig! See the snout out front? I wonder what it's carrying."

"Grain," answered the man standing on Kate's other side. "Or iron ore from the Mesabi Range. Could be either one."

He pointed to hatch covers bolted to the deck. "When she's fully loaded, waves wash right over her. In 1892 a ship like that took the first cargo of Minnesota ore down the Great Lakes— nine railroad cars full."

"One ship carried what was in nine railroad cars?" Anders asked.

"Yup. And now ships carry much more. *Whalebacks* are built right across the bay, other side of Connor's Point in Superior. You've heard about Alexander McDougall?"

Anders shook his head.

"He thought up the way to carry a lot of cargo in the least expensive way possible. When he first got the idea for a new kind of iron ship, people thought he was crazy."

Kate squirmed, thinking how she had made fun of the boat.

"His ships do have kind of a funny shape. Captain McDougall called 'em whalebacks. Lots of other people call 'em pig boats. But you know, McDougall is a shipbuilding genius."

As Kate looked back toward the bay, a large vessel with a pointed steel hull tooted its whistle. The engineer on the aerial bridge signaled back. The great freighter passed under the bridge and through the canal.

"Where do you think it's going?" Kate asked as the ship sailed into Lake Superior.

"Could be most anywhere on the Great Lakes."

As the freighter sailed off in the distance, Kate and the boys turned away from the canal. On the other side of the Corps of Engineers building, they saw a building with a large sign reading *Booth Fisheries*. Fishermen had tied up at a nearby slip, the open space between two piers for docking boats.

"Let's talk to those men," Erik said. "Maybe one of them saw something that would help us."

As he and Anders asked questions about Grandma, they discovered that many of the men were from Norway. Often the boys spoke Swedish to find out what they needed to know.

"What did he say?" Kate asked Anders as they left one of the fishermen.

"He asked, 'Why isn't that girl wearing a hat?' "

"A hat?" Kate clutched the top of her braid and felt the bow Betsy had given her.

Anders grinned, and Kate suspected that he was teasing her.

At the next fisherman they stopped again.

"What did he say?" Kate wanted to know as they walked on.

This time Erik answered. "Just one thing. 'How come you've got that cute girl with you?' "

A flush of embarrassment warmed Kate's cheeks.

Anders stopped a third fisherman as he left the building where fish were packed for shipment. This time Kate didn't bother to ask what the man said.

Anders told her anyway. "He wants to know, 'Who's that girl tagging along with you?' "

Kate stopped dead in her tracks. "Who's tagging along with *who*?"

The more questions the boys asked, the more upset Kate felt. All day long they'd been chasing dead ends, and Anders and

Erik were making a joke of it. Whenever they had come close to Grandma, she had slipped out of their reach.

After a time, Kate found a place with a good view of the bay and sat down to rest. As she and the boys watched, a tugboat towed an old wooden ship through the canal. The steamer had cargo piled twelve to fourteen feet high on the deck.

"What's it carrying?" Kate asked.

"Lumber," Erik told her. "The boards are stacked together really tight."

The large freighter towed three barges, also piled high with lumber. "Probably came from one of those sawmills." Anders pointed toward tall smokestacks in the bay.

Soon after the steamer passed into Lake Superior, the sun dropped behind the hills of Duluth. The choppy water in the bay grew black and flecked with foam.

At dusk a thick fog began to creep across the harbor. Silent and still, the fog soon hid anything more distant than the length of one of the big freighters. Kate felt the wetness against her face. Then she felt the coldness creep into her bones. She untied her coat from around her waist and pulled it on.

Erik stood up. "We need to get home."

Kate dreaded facing Grandpa and seeing the questions in his eyes. The day would have been even longer for him than for them.

"One more try," she pleaded. "Let's talk to that fisherman who just came in."

The man had dark brown hair, bushy eyebrows, and a beard trimmed close to his chin. His skin had weathered into a soft leather.

Kate showed him the carving. "It's my grandma, Emma Lindblom. A man stole her away from the immigrant room."

"Yah?" the man asked. The lines in his forehead deepened. "She's from the Old Country?"

"Sweden," Kate said.

"And a man stole her away?" He spoke with an accent, and Kate guessed that he came from Norway. "Why?"

"We don't know," Kate said. "She was wearing a fur coat—"

"A fur coat? An immigrant in a fur coat?"

"It was given to her," Kate explained quickly. "A reward. My grandpa saved a little boy's life."

"Ahhhh." The fisherman nodded with understanding. "And now someone needs to save your grandma's life."

"Have you seen her?" Kate asked. "She has white hair."

The man shook his head. "I would remember. If I see her, what should I do?"

"Try to watch where she goes," Anders said. "Tell the police."

The man nodded. "If I can do anything more to help, find me here. Ask for Captain Ole Hanson. How can I get hold of you?"

"We're staying with a woman named Marie Barclay," Anders told him.

"Marie Barclay?" The captain seemed even more alert. "How is she?"

"Her husband died a year ago," Kate said.

A strange look passed over the captain's face as though he grieved for Mrs. Barclay. Yet there was something more. Kate wondered what it was.

"I didn't know about his death," the captain said quietly. "Tell her I am sorry."

By the time Kate and Anders and Erik left the harbor, dusk had changed to darkness. Across the canal, the inner range light flashed. From the end of the south pier the outer light beckoned. As they walked toward the lighthouse, the foghorn groaned, paused a minute, then groaned again.

When they started up the nearest street, Kate saw the sign read *St. Croix Avenue.* She felt the need to hurry. "Grandpa will worry, and he doesn't need that."

Like gray cotton, the fog and darkness surrounded them. Soon after leaving the canal, Kate sensed a movement behind them. A strange movement she couldn't quite explain.

I'm getting jumpy, she thought. Yet she slipped between Anders and Erik and walked faster.

A block farther on, Erik stopped near a tall boardinghouse. "Do we know where we're going?" he asked.

"Sure," Anders answered. "Right up the street. Nothing to it."

But Kate caught a sound. Footsteps from behind them. Someone else was walking home in the night.

Turning around, she tried to see through the thick wall of fog. Instead, she felt closed in by a heavy smell. What was it?

Then Kate knew. The scent of cigar smoke.

Trying not to panic, she tugged at her brother's arm. Sniffing, she pointed back, then ahead.

Anders and Erik understood and picked up their pace. In another block Erik asked, "Where's Lake Avenue?"

"I think it's to our left," Kate answered. In the fog she felt unsure of everything.

"You betcha it's to our left." Anders sounded impatient. "It's the dividing line between avenues numbering east and west."

"I know. I was there when Mrs. Barclay explained." Erik turned at the next corner, and they walked until they found Lake Avenue. But soon Erik stopped. "Have we crossed Superior Street yet?"

Kate couldn't blame Erik for wondering. The fog swirled around them, seeming to grow deeper by the minute.

"We'll know when we do," Kate said. "Once we reach the other side of Superior Street, the hill goes up at a sharp angle."

She was still then, listening. *I don't hear any footsteps. Only the foghorn. Maybe whoever followed us is gone.*

Once more Erik started walking. As his long legs reached out, Kate did her best to stay with him. Behind them, the footsteps started again, the sound clear in the damp air.

Kate glanced around. Now she could see only as far as two buildings away. Kate grabbed Erik's arm, pointed back. "Listen," she mouthed without speaking aloud.

Erik nodded. "I know."

With head turned, Anders was also listening. As they hurried on, the boys took even bigger strides.

Soon Kate needed to run to keep up with their longer legs. Erik caught her hand, pulled her along. Each time they quickened their pace, the footsteps moved faster. When they slowed down, the person did not drop back.

Who could be following so close behind? Whoever it was, he no longer carried a cigar.

When they reached Superior Street, Erik turned left. The department store on the corner was closed for the night. So was everything else. And now Kate could see only seven or eight feet away.

Erik began running. In the gray-white world the footsteps started running too. The streetlights gave only a faint glow, adding to the strangeness of the night.

"Faster, Kate," Erik whispered.

"I can't!" she gasped, drawing long breaths.

Suddenly Erik jerked left, pulling Kate into a narrow opening between buildings. Anders followed.

Kate pressed back against the wall, trying to melt into the darkness. Huddled between the boys, she drew in great gasps of air. Then, afraid of making even a tiny sound, she stood motionless.

A minute later, footsteps pounded past them. For one fleeting instant, Kate saw a checked suit.

"It's that man!" she whispered. Her heart thudded with the terror of it. "Why is he following *us*?"

12

Christmas in May

I told you," Anders whispered back. "He wants to keep us from finding Grandma."

"But where is she now?" Kate asked, still speaking softly.

"Let's follow him and find out." Leaning down, Anders unlaced his boots and pulled them off. He tied the laces together and slung the boots over one shoulder.

Kate and Erik yanked off their shoes just as quickly. Then Anders ducked out of their narrow hiding place.

Kate followed him onto the sidewalk. As Anders leaped ahead, she ran after him, filled with dread that she'd fall behind.

Anders was used to going barefoot in summer, and he ran without making a sound. Kate tried to be just as quiet. A block and a half later, her brother angled across the street and started up the hill.

It seemed forever before they reached the next corner, but Anders ran on with Erik right behind. Kate's muscles ached as she tried to keep up with them.

Toward the end of the next block, Anders stopped to listen. Kate stopped too. Kate stopped too. The sound of footsteps faded, growing more distant.

"Stay here!" Anders whispered to Kate. "We can go faster."

"I'll keep up," Kate said, unwilling to be left alone.

"You can't. Erik and I have much longer legs."

Anders pointed to a narrow opening between two buildings. "Hide here and you'll be safe. We'll come back for you."

Before Kate could answer, he and Erik disappeared into the night. The fog surrounded Kate, closing in on her like a room with no way out.

The tall buildings had only a two-foot space between them. *Glass*, Kate thought, as she remembered her bare feet. *Broken glass.* Yet she was afraid to stand on the sidewalk all alone. In the murky darkness she slipped into the opening.

As the minutes grew long, Kate clutched her coat about her and stared out into the street. *Where's Anders? Where's Erik? What happened to them?*

From off in the distance the foghorn moaned. Kate strained her eyes, unable to see more than a few feet.

In the darkness beside her, she sensed a movement. She listened, but heard no sound. Then fur brushed against her ankle. Kate leaped away.

The furry body followed her. Again it brushed against her ankle. Kate held back a scream.

Then the animal stepped down on Kate's foot. An instant later, it meowed.

Kate felt silly. Glad that no one had seen her fear, she leaned against the brick wall and waited for her heart to stop pounding.

The cat meowed once more, then disappeared. In the stillness of the night, Kate wanted to call out, *Anders! Erik! Come back!* Instead, she peered into the street.

Again Kate saw nothing. But something was wrong—something other than the cat. In spite of her warm coat, Kate shivered. Fear walked in the fog and darkness.

Turning sideways, Kate gazed into the deeper darkness between the two buildings. Suddenly she stiffened.

At the far end of the narrow space, Kate saw a small red light. The light glowed, then faded, glowed again.

Even without sniffing, she knew what it was. How had the man found her hiding place?

On the back of Kate's neck her hair rose. Too afraid to move, she froze. In the fog the man must have escaped Anders and Erik. Somehow he had doubled back to slip between the two buildings at the opposite end.

Mean eyes, Kate thought. *The hack driver said he has mean eyes.*

Again she trembled. *If I leave, Anders and Erik won't find me.*

But there was more. *Which way is home?* In the gray-white fog she had lost all sense of direction.

Panic clutched Kate's stomach, moved up to tighten her throat. She strained to listen.

From the other end of the opening, she heard a noise. Had the man stumbled over something? If so, he was coming toward her.

Kate stared at the light of the cigar. Without making a sound, she slipped out of the opening onto the sidewalk. The terror within her growing, she started running.

No longer did she care about direction. She knew only that going downhill was easier than up.

But footsteps followed her. Faster and faster Kate ran, fleeing into the night.

Then a hand reached out, grabbed her arm.

"Kate, wait!" It was her brother's voice.

Kate stopped so suddenly that she almost lost her balance. In her relief, laughter bubbled up, spilled over.

"Shhhh!" Erik warned. A nearby streetlight showed the worry in his eyes.

Close to tears, Kate laughed again.

"Be quiet!" Anders commanded.

His words upset Kate even more. "Don't you shush me!" she said when she could speak. "We should have stayed together, and you left me!"

Kate's anger grew. "You lost him, didn't you? He found the same hiding place where you put me to be safe!"

Anders groaned. "Aw, Kate, I'm sorry. Bawl me out."

Kate opened her mouth again, but then she saw her brother's face. For over a year now, Anders had been her stepbrother. In all the times they had fought, in all the ways they had faced dangerous situations, Kate couldn't remember seeing Anders this upset. In that instant she knew how much he cared what happened to her.

"You're right," Anders said, his voice strangely humble. "It's my fault. We should have stayed together."

Kate knew her brother well enough to guess how much the apology cost him. Seldom had she been more surprised. Never had she appreciated him more.

"There's something that really bothers me," Kate said when they walked on. She ached with the thought of it. "What's happening to Grandma while that crook is running around?"

Neither of the boys could give an answer. At the next corner they found a street sign and decided which direction to take. Once more they started up the hill.

As they turned right at Second Street, Central High School rose from the darkness. The tall clock tower disappeared into the fog.

From a building across from the school Kate heard music—a band and singing. She recognized the tune: "What a Friend We Have in Jesus."

"I know that song!" she exclaimed, forgetting to be quiet.

Anders shushed her, and this time Kate didn't mind. She strained to hear. In contrast to the terror of the night, the music reached out like a special friend.

As they hurried on, the words grew more distinct. Then the music stopped. At a storefront building, Kate peered through the large window. They had come to a mission—a place where people could eat and sleep and attend a church service.

Men filled the rows of chairs set up on a scrubbed wooden floor. A young man in a Salvation Army uniform led the singing. When it started again, Kate heard a different tune.

Brightly beams our Father's mercy
From His lighthouse evermore;
But to us He gives the keeping
Of the lights along the shore.

"Listen!" Kate said. "That's the hymn Mrs. Barclay told me about!"

Let the lower lights be burning!
Send a gleam across the wave!
Some poor fainting, struggling seaman
You may rescue, you may save.

Like someone who had walked through a desert, Kate drank in each verse. When the singing stopped, the young man talked about the angry billows mentioned in the song.

I've never seen Lake Superior in a storm, Kate thought. *It must look the way I feel—all churned up inside.*

Standing there, she realized something. *I've been so busy searching for Grandma that I've forgotten God's love for me— me, Kate O'Connell—scared as I am. And God loves Grandma too. Whatever happens, He loves her even more than I do.*

For the first time since her frantic run through the night, Kate's fear slipped away.

Then Erik leaned close, whispered in her ear, "We have to go. Grandpa will be worried."

Kate turned away from the window. As they started up the steep hill, she felt still inside—even peaceful. Did that kind of peace also help people know what to do?

———

"Tell us everything that happened today," Grandpa said as they all gathered around the dining room table.

Mrs. Barclay sat at one end, filling plates with meat and potatoes and listening eagerly. Erik or Anders translated, and Grandpa clung to every word.

"You met Ole Hanson?" Mrs. Barclay asked. "How is he?"

"He was wondering the same thing about you!" Kate answered.

"I knew him when I first came to America—when I lived on Garfield Avenue."

Kate waited, hoping Mrs. Barclay would say more. Instead, their hostess suddenly pushed back her chair and went to the kitchen for another plate of meat.

Kate showed Grandpa the mittens they had found. He took the first, then the second one. Turning them over, he studied how they were made.

"Yah, this is my Emma's work," he said. "See how she knits the thumb? If one mitten is lost, the other will fit either hand."

"So that's where Mama learned!" Kate said. "She makes them the same way." More than once, two leftover mittens had become a new pair.

Grandpa stroked the soft red wool. "My Emma was making Christmas presents for each of you."

"When it's only May?" Kate asked.

"That is the way Emma is. She thinks ahead. All the way across the ocean she knitted mittens. I can't guess how many she's made by now. Probably a whole bagful!"

Grandpa's slow smile brought a twinkle to his blue eyes. "That man probably thinks he is stealing a bagful of gold. Most of it is mittens!"

For the first time since Kate had met him, Grandpa laughed out loud. The laughter spread across his face, creasing the lines around his eyes.

How can he laugh when Grandma's missing? Kate wondered. All she felt was heaviness.

But Grandpa grinned again. "You'll probably find mittens all over Duluth!"

This time Kate and the others joined in the joke. As the laughter died down, Grandpa wiped his eyes.

"My Emma is still—" He broke off, as though unwilling to say more.

Kate felt sure she knew what he was thinking: "She is still *alive.*"

13

More Questions

*T*hen Kate understood. *Grandpa needs to laugh. Is that what he learned during the hard times in Sweden?*

When everyone finished dessert, Kate brought the rest of the dishes out to the kitchen. As she set them down, she glanced through the partly opened window above the sink. The night air carried the scent of lilacs.

The scent reminded Kate of springtime in the country. Of tree frogs calling from every pond. For some reason Kate missed their noisy peeping. *Strange*, she thought. *Until Mama married Papa Nordstrom I always lived in the city.*

Then she knew what it was. Though she had lived there little more than a year, Windy Hill Farm was now home.

"Mrs. Barclay?" Kate asked as they worked together. "Why are you doing this for us?"

"Why did I bring you home with me?" Mrs. Barclay smiled. "When I was nineteen, I came from the Old Country—from Norway. I had no friends or relatives and didn't speak English. Then I worked as a maid in this house."

"A maid?" Kate asked, startled. "That's what Mama did. In a boardinghouse."

Mrs. Barclay nodded. A touch of gray lightened the hair around her face. "Then I became the housekeeper. A year after his first wife died, Mr. Barclay asked me to marry him."

She smiled. "It was unusual, I know. But my husband loved me. We had a good marriage until he died."

"Captain Hanson said to tell you that he's sorry about your husband," Kate said.

"Oh? He did?" Mrs. Barclay seemed surprised.

Her expression made Kate curious. "How well do you know Captain Hanson?"

"We were friends once—good friends." Mrs. Barclay's eyes grew soft. "We talked about getting married."

"What happened?" Kate asked.

Mrs. Barclay looked embarrassed. "We quarreled. It was my fault really. I sent him away. I never saw him again."

"He said that if he can do anything to help us, we should ask him."

"If you do need help, you can trust him," Mrs. Barclay said. "You can trust him, even with your life."

Early the next morning, Kate and Erik slipped out of the house.

"Where's Anders?" Kate asked as they started down to the canal.

"Still sleeping. I left him a note."

Kate felt impatient. "We need to get going."

"Going where?"

"Going anywhere we can find clues."

"Have you got some more to follow?"

Kate stared at him. "You know I don't!"

"Then what's your hurry? Where do you want to go?"

Kate stopped dead still, right in the midst of the sidewalk. "What's wrong with you?"

"Nothing's wrong with me."

"Yes, there is. We need to be doing something, and suddenly you talk about doing nothing."

Erik stopped too, facing her. "Kate, be reasonable. How can we go somewhere if we don't know where to go?"

But Kate was beyond listening. "For all your talk about grand-parents, it's not your grandma. It's *my* grandma. You just don't care enough!"

Erik sighed. "Kate, you know that's not true."

"If you cared more, you'd try harder."

"Kate, you're too tired. You don't even know what you're saying."

Kate drew herself up to her full height. "Is that so? So now I don't know what I'm talking about!"

"Aw, Kate, grow up!"

Kate flipped her long braid over her shoulder. "John wouldn't treat me the way you do. He'd *know* I'm grown up!"

"He'd know you're acting like a three-year-old instead of thir-teen!"

"Phooey!" Kate said.

Erik stalked off. Kate took her time about following. She knew she was wrong. She couldn't explain what had gotten into her, but she wasn't going to admit it, not for all the water in Lake Superior.

At the canal she finally let herself catch up to Erik. He stood at the end of the north pier, gazing south toward Minnesota Point. Along this side of the peninsula, a beach stretched away, as far as Kate could see.

For a long time she and Erik stood there, leaning against the concrete rail at the edge of the walkway. Across Lake Superior the deep red ball of the sun seemed to rise from the water.

Neither one of them spoke. Finally Erik turned. Kate could feel him gazing down at her, but she refused to look up.

"I know you're worried, Kate," he said quietly.

"You betcha!" Kate sounded like Anders.

"Well, first of all, we need to agree." Erik's voice changed. "We need to agree on what we want!"

Startled by the anger in his voice, Kate stared at him. "What do you mean?"

"I don't want to waste time telling you to stop running after a boy six years older than you, even if he is my own brother!"

Kate lifted her chin. "So what's it matter to you?"

"It matters a lot to me. I care about what happens to you."

"You do?" Kate felt a twinge of shame. She'd meant to tease Erik about John, not thinking it would really make any difference.

"I do." Erik's voice softened. "Kate, I like you. I like you a lot. In fact—"

Erik stopped. A slight flush colored his face.

Kate leaned forward, wishing he'd go on.

Before Erik could answer, Anders called to them. Erik stuffed his hands into his pockets and looked back to the open water.

"What's the matter, you two, sneaking off without me?" Anders asked when he reached them.

"Thought you needed to sleep," Erik answered. "You were snoring like a foghorn."

"Me? I don't snore. And I don't like being left behind."

Erik ignored him, and Kate looked out to the far horizon. The sunlight created a red path across the water.

"So?" Anders asked. "What do we do today?"

Kate looked at Erik. Erik shrugged.

"What do you say?" Anders sounded impatient. "Let's get moving."

Erik shook his head. "We've been doing too much of that. We've been running around like a chicken with its head cut off."

"Right!" drawled Anders. "Best we could manage."

"No, it's not!" Erik exclaimed. "We didn't rescue Grandma. And we don't have any more leads."

"So what do we do?" Anders asked when Kate remained quiet.

Erik turned to her. "You know those verses your mother read to us? They keep bothering me."

Kate knew what he meant. More than once she had felt the same way, but didn't want to admit it.

"We're supposed to ask in faith," Erik said. "Without doubting. Without wondering if we really want God's help."

"I'm so scared about Grandma, I can hardly think," Kate said. "How do we *not* doubt?"

Erik looked across the canal to the south pier. At the very end, set high above the surrounding water, was the lighthouse.

"By knowing where to look." Erik kept his gaze on the lighthouse. "Like sailors out at sea."

"Watching for the light," Kate said softly.

For a time she stood there, waiting for Erik to say more. When he didn't, she remembered the tower at Central High School. The idea of turning around had seemed so natural that she hadn't given it a second thought. After that, in the Spalding Hotel she had felt a nudge to look for an elevator. Was that what Erik meant about God helping them know what to do?

"Right now I feel uneasy," Erik said at last. "I've felt uneasy all morning. If we don't find Grandma soon, it will be too late."

"Too late?" Kate whispered.

Erik's face looked grim. "Even if that man doesn't hurt her, how long can she follow him around? She seems to be in awfully good shape for an older person. But how fast is he making her walk?"

Kate didn't like what she was hearing. "Grandpa says she's strong."

"But how strong?" Anders asked.

"If she's used to asking God for help, maybe she can handle more," Kate answered. "I hope so."

"So do I." But Erik's eyes looked troubled.

"Got any ideas about what to do?" Anders asked.

"Well—" Erik looked down at Kate as though afraid to say what he thought.

Kate squirmed under his gaze. She knew they couldn't expect to receive God's help when they were fighting. Yet she didn't want to give in—not even one half inch.

Then she thought of Grandma and their need to find her soon. She remembered Anders on the foggy street, actually admitting he had done something wrong.

"I'm sorry," Kate said to Erik.

"I'm sorry too," he answered.

"What's this all about?" asked Anders.

Kate turned away. She knew better than to give her brother more reasons to tease.

"Hmmmm," he said.

Kate stole a look at Erik and knew he was embarrassed. Yet he also knew better than to let Anders bait him.

"Something going on between you two?" Anders asked.

For a minute he was silent, as though trying to think something out. Suddenly he exploded. "So *that's* it!"

Her brother's voice was filled with such surprise that Kate looked up. Anders stared first at Erik, then at her.

"You know, when both of you grow up, you could get married."

14

Secret Trail

*O*h, *Anders!*" Kate was thoroughly embarrassed.

Erik choked. Again Kate turned away. As if her life depended on it, she gazed across the lake.

"I'm serious," Anders answered. "Wouldn't that be a good idea?"

"Sure, sure," Kate muttered.

Anders rattled on. "Now, why didn't I think of that before?"

"Probably 'cause it's up to Kate and me to think of it," Erik answered calmly.

Kate whirled around, afraid to look at Erik, yet longing to see his face. When she met his gaze, he smiled. Kate was the first to look away.

"We better figure out what to do about Grandma," she blurted out after a minute. Still embarrassed, Kate stumbled over the words.

Shielding his eyes against the growing sunlight, Anders stared at the horizon. "It's as if she vanished again! Do either of you have any ideas?"

Still feeling embarrassed, Kate hesitated. But her worry about

Grandma returned. As often before, Kate wondered, *What's happening to her right now?*

Erik moved restlessly. "I still feel uneasy." He seemed to read Kate's thoughts. "I think we're running out of time."

His words stripped away her fear of what Anders might say. "I think we should pray for wisdom again," Kate said. "Together, I mean." She wanted to agree on what they asked. She faced her brother. "Are you desperate enough to pray?"

"If we ask, we need to believe God answers," Erik added.

Anders stared at his friend. "All right," he said after a minute. "Grandma needs help, so I'll pray for wisdom." Anders started to bow his head, then looked up. "Don't worry, Kate, I'll mean it."

He spoke quickly, as though embarrassed to pray aloud. When he finished, they were silent, staring across the broad expanse of open water. On Lake Superior, long waves moved toward shore, driven by the wind. The waves broke against the pier, spraying upward.

"What *is* wisdom?" Kate asked as she watched the waves.

"The wisdom we need most is the one showing us what to do," Erik said.

Behind them, the high span of the aerial bridge stretched across the canal. The sun reached out toward the steel girders.

The air was still cool. Kate pulled her coat around her. "Right now I don't have any ideas about what to do. I just have one question!" She turned to her brother. "How come you never catch any fish?"

Anders looked at her as if she were crazy. "Well, I'm not a fisherman to start with!"

"I mean at home," Kate said. "On Rice Lake or Spirit Lake. Or the creek near the farm."

Anders rolled his eyes. "Sisters!"

Kate ignored him. "You remember what Papa said last summer?"

"Out of the countless things he said, what do you want me to remember?"

Kate snickered. "The time Papa asked, 'Do you know why

some people catch fish and some people don't? The people that catch them know how to think like a fish!' "

"So," Anders growled. "Can you please tell me what fishing has to do with finding Grandma?"

This time Kate laughed. "It's simple. If we're going to find a crook, we need to *think* like a crook!"

Anders stared at her. "You know, maybe you've got something there! It'd be like following a secret trail!"

"If you were the man who stole Grandma away, what would you do?" Kate asked.

"That's not hard to figure out. I'd have to lose anyone who tried to follow."

Erik grinned. "Which he managed to do."

"Then I'd have to think about hiding," Anders went on. "If that man planned ahead, he'd have a hideaway figured out. But how *could* he plan ahead? How would he know Grandma was going to come on the train? Grandma didn't know it herself!"

Erik looked thoughtful. "So the crook stole her away on the spur of the moment. That makes sense. But how does that explain a grudge? Remember the hack driver who talked about a man hanging around? Is he the same man as the person in the checked suit?"

Kate pushed a strand of hair out of her eyes. "The man told Grandma he knew his way around the school, so maybe he knows Duluth. But he probably doesn't live here. If he did, wouldn't he take Grandma to his house?"

"When he saw us following him, he needed another place to hide," Anders said. "That's the place we need to find!"

"He could hide." Kate pulled her braid forward and started twisting the end. "Or he could try to get out of the area."

"Which is it?" Erik asked. "We've got to think like a crook."

"If I knew the police were looking for me, I'd try to get out of Duluth," Kate said.

"So would I!" Anders exclaimed. "He could leave on a train."

"Or a boat." Kate watched a fisherman pass through the canal. "Or he could rent a hack again."

"Well, we can't look inside every house in Duluth and Superior," Erik said. "So let's ask around at the places where a crook could leave."

"Let's go to Union Depot first," Anders answered. "Grandpa asked me to turn in his train tickets. Then we'll have some money."

Inside the large room on the main floor, Kate stood in one ticket line, and the boys waited in the other two.

When Kate reached the ticket agent, she held up the carving of Grandma. "Have you seen anyone who looks like this?"

The agent shook his head.

"She would be with a man—a tall man in a checked suit."

Again the agent shook his head. Finally Kate turned away.

The boys did no better. As they went back outside, Anders stopped near the large arched doors. "Let's try the hacks again."

They found Tony with the other drivers. He flashed a welcoming smile, but answered no to their questions.

"I've been looking for your grandma," he said to Kate. "I told all the other drivers to keep a sharp watch. She hasn't been around since I took her up the hill. Sorry."

From there they walked to every livery stable in the downtown area, asking about carriage rentals. Each time, the person in charge shook his head.

"We asked God for help," Anders said as they came out of the last stable. "Why isn't He showing us what we need to know?"

"Sometimes He answers right away," Erik told him. "Other times it takes longer."

"Well, this is sure one of the longer times!" Anders exclaimed.

"The police station isn't far from here," Kate said. She tried to push aside the dread she felt whenever she thought about Grandma. "Maybe Sergeant Holmquist knows something more."

Soon they found the brownstone building on Superior Street. The sergeant asked them to tell him all that had happened since they had seen him. "I don't want to take a chance on missing anything," he said. "If the man has a grudge, what would it be?"

No one had any ideas.

When Anders told about Grandma leaving the Spalding Hotel, Sergeant Holmquist asked, "I wonder why the man took her there?"

Kate and Erik looked at each other. They both looked at Anders.

"We thought he was trying to lose anyone who might follow him," he said. "Kinda dumb, huh?"

"Not dumb," the sergeant said. "You've done a good job of tracking down leads. But the man could have stayed in hiding and didn't. He took a big risk to go that close to Union Depot."

Kate closed her eyes, trying to think. Something tugged at her memory. In the moment when she stared down at Grandma, Kate had seen something else—something off to one side. What was it?

Kate just couldn't bring it to mind. She thought of Grandpa and wished she could remember more.

"We'll keep doing everything we can," Sergeant Holmquist promised as they finished talking. "Meanwhile, you're chasing trouble. Don't take any chances. Stay together."

After her scare of the night before, Kate welcomed the reminder. His words seemed strangely familiar. As she and Anders and Erik left the station, Kate realized why. "He sounds just like Mama," she said.

———

All of them were used to walking long distances. Even so, they felt tired and discouraged as they started up the hill. When they reached Mrs. Barclay's house, Kate helped fix a middle-of-the-morning breakfast.

Mrs. Barclay led them to a small table outside the kitchen door. "I like being outdoors when the weather is good," she said.

Above the trees and lilac bushes at the back of the yard, the ground rose steeply to another level and a house farther up the hill.

As they gathered around the table, Grandpa put aside a carving he had started. "It helps me pass the time until we find

Grandma," he explained. Again he wanted to know everything that had happened.

Kate had her own questions. "Yesterday when I called from the roof, Grandma looked up, and I saw her face. Do you think she understood my words?"

When Erik translated, Grandpa nodded. Through Erik, Grandpa explained. "My Emma knows the English word *Grandma*, just like I understand when you call me Grandpa." He reached out and patted Kate's hand.

Erik and Anders told Grandpa about their visit to the police station.

"Trouble?" he said at last. "Sergeant Holmquist expects you will have trouble?"

Anders nodded, his gaze honest before Grandpa's steady look. "I'm afraid so."

"I am praying," Grandpa answered. "I am praying for your protection, the way I pray for my Emma."

He turned to Kate. "You know how much my Emma means to me." The old man's eyes seemed filled with pain. "But I want a promise from you. Don't put yourself in danger for her sake or mine."

But we need to catch that man! Kate avoided Grandpa's eyes.

"No foolish risks!" he said and waited for Kate to answer.

Kate hesitated. She didn't want to do anything foolish. Yet there might be risks in finding Grandma. What would be a real risk? What would be foolish, even dangerous?

But Grandpa would not let it go. "No foolish risks!" he said again.

"No foolish risks!" Kate finally promised, knowing she had no choice. Yet she felt uneasy again. What were the risks they might need to take in order to rescue Grandma?

As though reading her mind, Grandpa smiled at Kate. "You are very like my Emma."

It was almost as if Grandpa knew that something dangerous was going to happen.

15

Upside-Down Flag

*J*ust then a pigeon landed on the lawn only a few feet from where the family sat. As though unafraid, it tipped its slate-blue head to one side.

A moment later, another pigeon landed inside the high net fence at the back of the yard. Like the first pigeon, this one also had blue checks across its wing feathers. It, too, seemed without fear.

"They're really tame," Anders said.

"My husband was a pigeon fancier," answered Mrs. Barclay. "He liked them so much, I haven't had the heart to sell them. Even if I did, the older ones would keep coming back. They're homing pigeons."

"Homers?" Anders asked. "How did your husband train them?"

Mrs. Barclay seemed pleased by his interest. "When the pigeons were very young, he started by leaving a door in the loft open." She nodded toward the small building inside the fence.

"The pigeons went outside enough to know where their home is. As soon as they learned to fly, my husband took them a short distance away to see if they would come back.

"The next time he took them out, he doubled the distance. He kept doing that until they were trained to come home, even from many miles away. Homers are known to travel hundreds of miles."

As soon as they finished eating, Mrs. Barclay showed them the loft with its small trapdoors for returning pigeons.

"How do you tell them apart?" Kate asked.

Reaching up, Mrs. Barclay caught one of them. "See this tiny piece of metal around its leg? When the pigeons were very young, my husband banded them. Every homing pigeon has its own registered number. If a pigeon lands at the wrong place, the owner of that loft can contact me through the registration."

Anders held out his hand, and a pigeon landed on it.

"I see you like birds," Mrs. Barclay said. "It was my husband's hobby, but pigeons are useful too. Have you seen the huge rafts of logs that steamers tow across Lake Superior?

"They go to Ashland, Wisconsin, or all the way to Baraga, Michigan. My husband used to supply pigeons for ships like that. If a steamer had trouble, the men could release pigeons to ask for help."

As though just thinking of something, Mrs. Barclay turned to Anders. "Sergeant Holmquist warned you about trouble, didn't he? Would you like to take along some pigeons?"

Anders grinned. "Yah, sure, you betcha. Even if we don't need help, it'd be fun to see what they do."

"You can release them all at once, or one at a time."

Mrs. Barclay caught three pigeons and put them in a wicker basket. She gave Kate a small container for water and filled another container with bird food—a mixture of wheat and peas and corn.

Then Mrs. Barclay took out some small tubes. "Just roll up your message and put it inside." She showed them how to attach the tube to a pigeon's leg.

"When you let one of them go, hold it like this." Mrs. Barclay held the pigeon up, then opened her hands.

"If there's a bad storm, a pigeon might have trouble finding its way. Otherwise, it will head straight for home. When you're gone, I'll keep a sharp lookout and get help right away."

When Kate, Anders, and Erik left the house again, they took along the three pigeons.

"Just in case," Erik said grimly.

Kate carried the smaller basket with food. As they walked down the hill, she looked at her brother—really looked at him. Anders seemed restless and as frustrated as she felt.

"Grandpa's treasure!" Kate exclaimed. "What's going to happen to Grandpa if we don't find Grandma? It's bad enough for us. Just think how he must hurt inside."

"Just think how Ben will feel," Anders said. "If we don't find Grandma, he'll blame himself."

Kate had already thought of the same thing. In the short time she had known him, Kate had grown to love her nineteen-year-old uncle. More than once, he had been a friend to her and Anders.

"There's something we still don't know," she said. "Why did that man go to the Spalding Hotel?"

"That's also the place where we found our last good clue," Erik answered. "Since we don't know what else to do, why don't we go there?"

When the three entered the hotel lobby, they saw fashionably dressed people hurrying in and out. Off to one side stood a girl about Kate's age. She wore a sailor hat—a flat-topped straw hat with a wide black ribbon around the crown and a streamer that hung down her back.

Kate couldn't help but steal a look at Anders.

"She's wearing a hat!" he said.

Kate made a face, then ignored his teasing. Looking around, she tried to take in everything. Suddenly it dawned on her. "So that's why Grandma wears the fur coat! No one else is wearing one!"

Erik grinned. "She wants to get noticed! I bet she pretends that she's cold."

Kate laughed. Yet her good feelings faded quickly, replaced by worry. All the beautiful wood paneling seemed to close in on her. "Why did the man bring Grandma to the hotel? When she dropped the mitten next to the elevator, Grandma must have thought she was going up."

Again a memory tugged at the corner of Kate's mind. Something she should put together.

"So what was their reason for going up?" Erik asked. "They couldn't have stayed very long."

"But long enough to meet another person," Anders said.

"That's what it was!" Kate exclaimed.

She remembered looking down from the roof of the Spalding. The man walked next to the street, clutching Grandma's right arm. But there was someone else—someone nearby. "There was a woman with them!"

"You're sure?" Erik asked.

"Positive. I was so excited about seeing Grandma, my mind didn't take it in. The man was carrying a small suitcase."

"I thought you said he had his hand on Grandma's elbow."

Kate turned to Anders. "He did. His other hand held the suitcase."

"Can you describe the woman?" Erik asked.

Kate struggled to think. "Brown hair. But I didn't see much more than the top of her head. When I called to Anders, she turned, just for a second. Maybe I'd recognize her if I saw her again."

Then Kate realized something else. Like a cold hand, a fist seemed to tighten around her heart. "There are two people watching Grandma now."

Feeling as if she needed more air, Kate hurried out the nearest door. She came out on Fifth Avenue West, the street along the side of the hotel.

"It was around the corner," she said as Anders and Erik followed her.

When they reached Michigan Street, Kate looked up the back side of the hotel. Far above was the railing for the covered walkway. They were standing close to where Grandma had walked.

This time they searched the area even more carefully. Finally Anders said, "It's no use, Kate. There's nothing here but sidewalk."

"But when I called, Grandma looked up. Grandpa says she knows the English word for Grandma."

"What are you saying, Kate?" Anders asked.

"I know," Erik answered for her. "Grandma was leaving a trail before she knew that someone was following. At Central High School she probably caught a glimpse of Kate in the auditorium. After that, she'd try even harder to leave a trail."

"But now there's a difference," Anders said. "Grandma has probably guessed that we'll look hard for a clue. We don't have to be able to stumble over it."

Kate started back to Fifth Avenue. "A fur coat must have pockets. If Grandma put mittens in her pockets, it'd be easier to drop them without being noticed."

"But when she left here, she had two people watching what she dropped," Anders said.

"So she'd have to be even more careful." Once again, something tugged at Kate's mind.

In that instant, she knew what it was. "I thought Grandma and the man left through the back door. They could have gone out the side just like we did!"

Kate stood at the back corner of the hotel. As she looked along the side wall, she saw that the windows in the bottom row were small, as though for a basement. The top of the glass was only a few feet above the sidewalk.

"The window wells!" Kate yelped.

She hurried over next to the building. At each window, she looked down into the empty space that held dirt away from the glass. In the fourth window well Kate found what she was looking for. "Another mitten!"

Feeling she had discovered gold, Kate picked it up. Like the other mittens, this one was knitted with red wool yarn. It could also fit either a left or right hand. But this mitten was exactly Kate's size.

As she slipped her hand inside, Kate felt something. A piece of paper! She pulled it out.

The paper was folded three times. "A message!" Kate said as she opened it. "Look!"

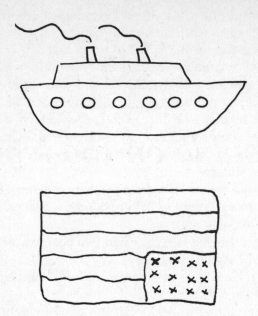

Kate had no doubt that the first picture was a ship. But the second one?

"An American flag?" Kate asked. She stared at what could be stars and stripes. The lines wobbled, as if drawn by a trembling hand.

"Grandma wouldn't have time to make forty-five stars," Erik said.

The longer Kate looked at the drawing, the more upset she felt. "Do you think she knows the meaning of an upside-down flag?"

16

Trouble on the North Shore

$\mathcal{A}$nders looked away as though he didn't want to answer Kate's question. But Erik faced her, his gaze steady.

"Grandma probably knows it's a distress signal," Erik said quietly. "I think it's an international signal for someone in trouble."

The paper shook in Kate's hand. "I'm so scared," she said, her voice barely above a whisper. "So far Grandma has seemed calm—as if she knew what she was doing. But not now. What makes it worse, this drawing is two days old!"

"We need someone smarter than we are," Anders said. "Let's find Captain Hanson."

Kate tucked the message back into the mitten. With Anders still carrying the basket of pigeons, they hurried to the canal.

The waterfront was busy with returning fishermen. They found Captain Hanson tying up his seventy-foot boat, the *Sea Gull*. The pilothouse was near the bow, or front of the boat. From there a roof extended to the stern or back of the boat. Beneath

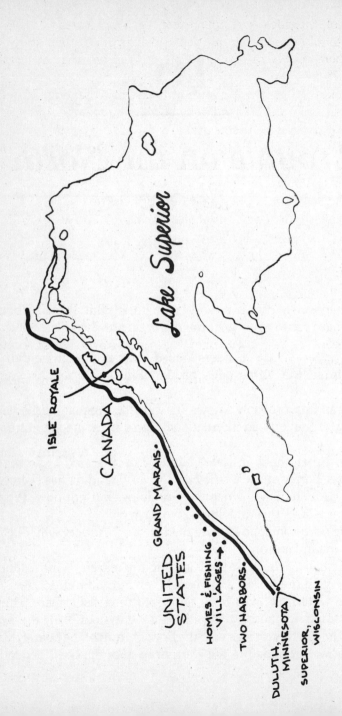

Lake Superior

ISLE ROYALE

CANADA

UNITED STATES

GRAND MARAIS

HOMES & FISHING VILLAGES →

TWO HARBORS

DULUTH, MINNESOTA

SUPERIOR, WISCONSIN

that roof, the sides were open except for a small area.

Kate told the captain all that had happened, then showed him their newest discovery. "Can you tell us what this note means?"

He needed only one glance at Grandma's drawing. "Could be a distress signal. Or maybe she heard talk about the *America*."

"The *America*?" Anders asked.

"The steamer owned by Booth Fisheries. It goes up the North Shore to Isle Royale and Canada. Big boat, it is—185 feet long. Looks like a palace."

"And someone could get a ride?" Erik asked.

"It takes passengers and mail and collects fish."

"Did the *America* leave this morning?"

"Nope. Sailed out yesterday. You said you saw the man last night in the fog?"

Erik nodded.

"Then Kate's grandma can't be on board. But a smaller boat could have taken them. On the other side of Two Harbors the road leaves the lake. If that man wants to go up the North Shore, he'd have to go by water."

Captain Hanson looked around. "Let me ask some questions."

Walking up and down the pier, he talked to the other men. Before long, he motioned for Kate and the boys to come over.

"I saw a man and older lady this morning," a fisherman said. "She seemed spry enough. But when they climbed into a fishing boat, the man had a good hold on her elbow, like he was helping her."

"Forcing her into the boat!" Kate muttered to Anders.

"Lady tried to talk to me," the fisherman went on. "But the man said, 'You know, she's not thinking real clear. Sometimes she gets it into her head that I'm going to hurt her. All I'm trying to do is help.' He hurried her onto the boat."

Kate's stomach churned. "What did she look like?"

"Wearing a fur coat. Looked mighty swell for a ride in an old tub."

"Do you have any idea where they went?" asked Captain Hanson.

"Up the North Shore."

Kate shrunk back, afraid to hear anything more.

The fisherman noticed. "What's the matter, young lady?"

"She's my grandmother," Kate answered. She felt as if her heart were bleeding.

"Sounds like you've got serious trouble," Captain Hanson said as they walked back to his boat.

"Where would that awful man take her?" Kate asked.

Pushing back his visored cap, the captain scratched his head. "I don't know. There are hundreds of fishing stops between here and Isle Royale. I collect fish north of the city of Two Harbors."

Kate bit her lip. Once away from Duluth, what would happen to Grandma? How much time did they have?

"Tell you what," Captain Hanson said. "You boys look like you can handle hundred-pound kegs. Give me a hand unloading. Then I'll take you up the Shore a ways."

The deck of the *Sea Gull* was loaded high with wooden kegs filled with fish. Anders lifted one down, then rolled it along the pier into the fishery. Erik followed with another keg.

When the deck was clear, Captain Hanson raised what he called a hatch. As he swung back the cover, Kate saw an opening into the hold. There the rest of the cargo was stored.

After a great number of trips, all of the kegs were inside the fish-packing building. As soon as the *Sea Gull* was ready, Captain Hanson told Kate, "Hop in!"

Kate hung back. "I just remembered Grandpa and Mrs. Barclay. We better tell them where we're going."

"No problem." The captain hurried into the building and returned with a young man. "Write a note, and Willie will swing around on his way home to Connor's Point."

When Kate climbed on board, Captain Hanson led her into the pilothouse. Windows filled the front and two sides, giving a good view of the harbor.

At the stern of the *Sea Gull* there was a cabin—a small room across the width of the boat. Anders set the baskets with the pigeons and food there. Then he joined Erik in leaning against the doorway on the back side of the pilothouse.

Standing at the large wooden wheel, the captain eased the *Sea Gull* out of the slip. Soon they passed through the canal into the gently rolling swells of Lake Superior.

"I'm what you call a collection boat," the captain explained as they started up the North Shore. "I slow down at a village or give a whistle. Men sell me their fish—frozen whole and put in sacks during winter, or salted, in kegs like you saw, in summer. I take the fish into Duluth."

Captain Hanson waved his hand toward the shoreline. "Fisherman-farmers live all along here. Fish from the sea, farm from the land. I bring 'em supplies—milk, nets, whatever they need."

At the first village where they slowed down, a dock extended into Lake Superior. Near a log house, large racks held nets drying in the sun.

When Captain Hanson tooted his whistle, a man came out of a shed. He jumped into a long, narrow boat and rowed out.

"It's too shallow to take the *Sea Gull* in," the captain said, "but that skiff can come out here." He cupped his hands around his mouth and called, "Have you seen a white-haired lady along here?"

When the fisherman shook his head, Captain Hanson waved and went on. In a stretch of deep blue water the *Sea Gull* drew close to another skiff. Like the first one, it was pointed on both ends.

"Whichever way it goes—into shore or out—the skiff heads right into the waves," the captain said. "No water splashing over a square stern."

Captain Hanson swung out, then slowed the engine. The fisherman was passing a net across the bow. Working quickly, he picked fish from the net, emptying them into his boat.

Again the captain explained. "He's using a gill net to catch herring. Fish gills catch on the net, and they can't get back out. But the smaller herring—the ones that should grow for a while—swim through without being caught."

He called to the fisherman. When the man shook his head, the *Sea Gull* moved on.

Kate eyed the gently rolling waves. "Have you been out in really bad storms?"

The captain nodded. "More than I'd like. Storms come up sudden on Lake Superior. Even though you're careful, you can get caught at the wrong time."

"I heard someone talking about the Mataafa Blow," Anders said.

"Worst storm in the history of Lake Superior." The captain shook his head, as though still unable to believe it. "November 1905. Less than two years ago. Eighteen ships destroyed or damaged. At least thirty-four men died in all. Strangest nor'easter we ever had."

"What do you mean, a nor'easter?" Kate asked.

"Wind blows from the northeast, all the way across the lake. In Duluth that's 250 miles." Beneath bushy brows, the captain's eyes scanned the horizon.

"Sea conditions depend on a lot of things," Captain Hanson said. "Strength of the wind, length of time it blows, and the distance it covers. Depth of water makes a difference too. Near Duluth the water is more shallow than in the middle of the lake. When waves blow into shallow water, they crest and break. That's when they're the most dangerous."

Along the shore, water crashed against huge rocks, spraying upward. From a cloudless sky the sun shone brightly. Toward the northeast, deep blue water stretched away as far as Kate could see.

As the *Sea Gull* drew near another village, the captain slowed down and tooted his whistle. When they went on again, he kept talking.

"In 1905 a nor'easter started on the twenty-third of November, and captains stayed in port. When the weather got better, everyone steamed out on the lake. There's usually a time of good weather after a nor'easter. But three days after the first storm, an even bigger one hit. Winds blew at least sixty miles an hour for more than twelve hours. Snow, and ice, and terrible cold. Sailors tell me the waves seemed higher than a smokestack.

"A steel freighter called the *Mataafa*—430 feet long—tried to get back to Duluth. She was just ready to slip into the canal when a wave slapped her against the north pier. Waves kept beating her—turned her sideways to the canal and ran her aground.

"There she was—just a few hundred feet off shore. Crowds of people from Duluth stood on shore, wanting to help."

Captain Hanson pounded his fist against the wheel. "The boys from the life saving service did everything they could. Fishermen wanted to go out. I was one of 'em. But we couldn't get to her!

"Nine men died. One of them was my friend. There was nothing I could do."

For a time the captain was silent, his bearded jaw firm, his eyes straight ahead.

"Maybe you can't imagine a storm like that," he said at last. "Not unless you know something else."

Again his eyes scanned the horizon. "At the beginning of the blow, the assistant keeper got out to the Duluth lighthouse. Kept the light and the foghorn going all through the storm.

"Captain Prior, the main keeper, tried to reach him. Tried to use the tunnel built under the south pier for just that reason. But the tunnel was flooded by high seas.

"Twice Captain Prior tried to walk out to the lighthouse. Both times waves crashed over and washed him off the pier. It took him two hours to clear the ice from the door of the inner range light. But he kept it going."

Again Captain Hanson shook his head. "That's why we call it the Mataafa Blow."

Nine men died? At the end of the pier? Kate ached with the thought of it. She glanced back to Anders and Erik and saw their eyes.

Now with sunlight dancing across the water, Lake Superior was at its best. *Blue and beautiful,* Kate decided. Then another thought struck her. *Cold and deep.*

She felt glad this was May, not November, glad for the captain's experience on Lake Superior.

Then he spoke again. "November is our worst month, but storms come up any time of the year."

His hands tightened on the wheel. "The lake is my friend, but it's a harsh master."

More than three hours later, the *Sea Gull* reached the city of Two Harbors. A breakwater—a long wall of rocks—extended from the north toward the opening into the harbor.

"See how it's built?" asked Captain Hanson. "Protects the harbor from nor'easters."

A second breakwater reached out almost at a right angle to the first. The captain turned the *Sea Gull* into the narrow opening between the two walls. He tied up alongside other fishing boats.

Here, too, Captain Hanson asked questions, but without success. Soon they went on. Time after time, a man, and once a woman, rowed out to talk to the captain.

As they left yet another fishing village, Kate said, "I'm sorry. We're wasting your time."

Captain Hanson shook his head. "Nothing's wasted when it's someone you care about."

Once more he tooted his whistle. A man along the shore leaped into his skiff and rowed out.

When the captain asked about a white-haired lady, the fisherman looked uneasy. "Why do you want to know?"

Captain Hanson nodded toward Kate. "It's her grandmother, stolen away from Union Depot in Duluth."

The man swore. "I told—" He broke off, as though realizing he had given himself away.

"What do you know?" the captain asked quickly.

The man's fists tightened. He glanced at Kate, then away.

"Would you like to tell me or someone else?" The captain's voice had steel running through it.

The fisherman shot him a resentful look, then seemed to think it over. "The wife says a woman was here when I was out fishing this morning."

"You saw her?" Kate asked.

"Nope. The wife talked to her."

"Who's the man with her?" asked the captain.

"My wife's brother," the fisherman said. "The wife don't want him around. She's scared of him—*real* scared."

17

Two Harbors Breakwater

*G*et your wife," Captain Hanson said.

Again the fisherman seemed to debate with himself. Then without another word, he rowed back to shore. Minutes later, he returned with a woman in the boat.

The captain threw a line. The fisherman caught it and tied the skiff to the *Sea Gull*.

"Better tell me what you know," Captain Hanson said to the woman.

Sitting with head bowed, she stared at her hands.

"I'd like to hear your side of the story," the captain went on.

Between nervous fingers, the woman twisted the corner of her apron. "I don't want to tell on my brother."

"When he does something wrong, you don't have to defend him," the captain said. "You'll hurt your brother more if you let him keep on with what he's doing."

The woman glanced sideways at her husband. When he nodded, she seemed to gather courage. "He's a bad one, my brother

Jonas is—in trouble with the law since knee-high to a grasshop-
per."

"What did the woman look like?" Kate asked.

"Tall lady, white hair."

Kate held up Grandpa's carving. "Like this?"

The woman's gaze darted toward the carving. Finally she
nodded. "Walked like a—" She paused, as though searching for
the right word. "Like a queen, she was. Wearing a fur coat. When
I saw the coat and the lady, I asked Jonas, 'What you tryin' to
do now?'

" 'Just want to stay a few nights,' he said.

"Right away I figured that one out. He wants to collect big
money and leave the blame on me.

" 'You'll get us into trouble,' I said. 'That's what you'll do.' "

For the first time, the fisherman's wife looked the captain
straight in the eye. "When Jonas went outside for a minute, the
lady started talking Swede. I'm Norwegian, and I understood."

"What did Grandma tell you?" Kate asked.

"She said, 'He told me my husband was hurt. Jonas took me
to the hospital. Then he said, 'I've taken your husband. If you
make trouble, I'll hurt him?'

"When Jonas came back, he told the lady to shut up. I said,
'I don't want nothing to do with your mess!' I never stood up to
him before, and he looked surprised. 'You take care of this lady,'
I said. 'If you hurt her, you're in trouble the likes of which you
never seen!' "

"What did your brother do?" the captain asked.

"He took the lady back to the boat they came on."

Kate sighed. Once again they had missed Grandma. "Do you
think Jonas went to another fishing village?"

The woman shook her head. "Honest folk won't take 'em in.
It's clear as the nose on your face what he's trying to do. By now
they're back in Duluth."

"Where?" Erik's question shot out like a bullet.

The woman kept her gaze on Kate, but she no longer twisted
her apron. "Don't know. When Jonas gets into trouble, he holes
up till it blows over."

"Any certain place he likes to hide?" Anders asked.

The woman shook her head. "He used to have a string of 'em. But he never told me where they were. He's been in and out of jobs a long time. Don't want to work. Never gets along with no one. Don't know how Stella puts up with it."

"Stella?" Erik asked.

"His wife. He met her somewhere in Duluth and has to go back for her."

"Thank you," Kate said as Captain Hanson untied the line between boats. "Thank you very much!"

"Don't tell my brother you seen me." The woman looked like a cornered animal. "Don't tell him you talked to me. I'm scared of what he might do."

As Captain Hanson turned the *Sea Gull* toward Duluth, the lake was calm, the water smooth as glass. Kate, Anders, and Erik went back to the cabin.

Built across the width of the boat, the space was about ten feet deep. An old coffeepot sat on the coal stove used for cooking meals. Dishes and groceries filled the shelves—a bag of lump sugar, another bag of coffee, and a loaf of bread. Portholes on the two side walls gave a good view of the lake.

The door of the cabin opened toward the front of the boat. Kate looked across the long deck and the raised hatch to the pilothouse. Captain Hanson had left his door open, and she could see him standing at the wheel.

Kate sat down on one of the benches and leaned back, enjoying the beauty of the great lake. For a time she watched the waves crash against the rocks along the shore. Always Kate had liked water and never more so than now.

"Well, we've got some answers," Erik said. "Jonas's name and the reason he went to the Spalding Hotel—to meet his wife."

"But we still don't know where he is." Just the same, Kate felt hopeful again. *We'll find Grandma this time. If only we get there before Jonas hurts her!*

Soon Kate walked forward to stand inside the pilothouse

again. The *Sea Gull* was making good time toward Duluth when the captain said, "So you're staying with Marie Barclay."

"She's been very kind to us." As Kate answered, she watched his eyes. "Even though we're strangers, she's taken us into her home."

"That sounds like Marie. How is she doing?" he asked, as he had before.

Kate grinned. "She wondered the same thing about you."

Watching him, Kate felt sure that she knew what the captain wanted to know. "Should I tell her you have a wife and family?"

Captain Hanson tried to look stern. Instead, his eyes twinkled. "You can tell her I never married."

The captain stood sideways, turning often to look around the lake. After a time, Kate noticed there was something different about the way he watched. Still with his hand on the wheel, Captain Hanson stared back over his left shoulder.

As he studied the far reaches of Lake Superior, Kate's gaze followed his. She saw a strange black line along the northeast horizon.

"What is it?" she asked.

The captain's hands tightened on the wheel. "Bit of a storm."

He called to the boys. "Stay inside the cabin. Don't try to cross the deck."

The black line moved closer and closer. Within minutes the sun disappeared, replaced by heavy overcast. Driven by the wind, the calm seas changed to great swells of water. The waves caught the *Sea Gull*, sweeping it forward.

When the boat stood on the crest of a wave, Kate saw for miles. Then the boat slipped down into a trough. Green waves rose in mountains, surrounding them. Everywhere Kate looked, there was water. At first she liked the movement of the boat rushing through the waves. As though pushed by a giant hand, the *Sea Gull* ran before the wind.

Soon Kate's excitement slipped away. She stared at the churning water, green now instead of blue, and flecked with foam. As a wall of rain struck the boat, her stomach tightened.

Great sheets of water pounded down upon them. Waves

crashed over the open deck, ran alongside the raised hatch. Looking back, Kate saw Anders slam the door of the cabin.

Then powerful winds struck them. Waves rose in even higher mountains. As the boat rocked up and down, Kate stared at the swells. *One of the coldest lakes in the world*, people say. *How long would we last in the water?*

Kate pushed the question away and tried to think about finding Grandma. The *Sea Gull* rode down into another trough, then up on a crest. Within half an hour, eight-foot swells surrounded the boat.

"Will you land along here?" Kate asked the captain. Through the driving rain she tried to see the shore.

"The water isn't deep enough. Smaller boats can go in and out, but I can't."

Not deep enough, Kate thought, the fear within her growing. She remembered the captain's words: "In shallow water waves crest and break. That's when they're the most dangerous."

Now Kate thought of something else—the rocks along the shore.

Before long, the swells ran fifteen feet high. Each wave seemed to last forever. As if her life depended on it, Kate watched the captain.

His knuckles white, he grasped the wheel. Each time the seas flung them forward, he kept the bow straight. The waves battered the stern.

After a time, Kate realized what he was doing. The captain didn't want to let a wave catch him sideways. *The Mataafa!* she thought. *Slammed against a pier!*

"I'll put in at Two Harbors," the captain said.

As if in a bad dream, Kate remembered the breakwaters sheltering the harbor. When they reached the mouth of the harbor— the opening between the great rocks—they needed to turn. All of Kate's other fears fell away before one question. *What if a wave hits us broadside?*

Her panic growing, she wondered about Anders and Erik. *What's happening to them?*

Then through the slashing rain, Kate saw the breakwater. Just inside lay Two Harbors.

Pushed before the wind, the *Sea Gull* sailed down the long line of rocks, heading southwest. As the boat drew close to the harbor mouth, a great wave crashed upon them.

A second wave followed the first, hitting the stern. The boat shuddered, leaped forward.

As though waiting for a safe moment, Captain Hanson clenched the wheel. The *Sea Gull* slid past the opening.

Kate groaned. Had they missed their only hope?

Then in an instant of calm, the captain turned the boat at a right angle. The bow of the *Sea Gull* pointed toward the mouth of the harbor.

Out of nowhere, a wall of green water bore down upon them. Seconds later, it struck them broadside. Kate felt the boat tip!

18

Bad News

*A*s the *Sea Gull* leaned over, Kate fell on her side. Her heart pounded with terror.

Then the boat settled back in the water, right side up. As Kate scrambled to her feet, the *Sea Gull* slipped behind the breakwater. With his gaze straight ahead, Captain Hanson still held the wheel.

"We're safe now," he said. In the calmer waters he loosened one hand from the wheel, flexed his fingers. But Kate saw his eyes and knew that he, too, felt shaken.

As Captain Hanson tied up at the pier, Kate ran back to the cabin. When she flung open the door, she found broken dishes scattered across the floor. Sugar lumps, coffee grounds, and bread was mixed with coal and glass.

Erik and Anders were still getting to their feet, but they hurt. Kate's knees felt wobbly with relief.

When Anders saw her, he tried to make a joke of what had happened. But Kate knew the truth. Her brother's face looked gray-white.

When they were all ashore, a fisherman's family took them in for the night. "It's a miracle!" the man told Captain Hanson. "A miracle that you're all right!"

Sometime during the night Kate woke to rain still pounding against the roof. With dawn the rain and high winds continued.

All morning Kate stared out a window, more restless than she had ever been in her life. What was happening to Grandma while they were here, unable to leave Two Harbors?

"If only we could get back to Duluth," Kate whispered to Anders and Erik. Already her memory of the storm had faded. She feared for Grandma more. Every minute of waiting seemed like ten hours.

At noon Captain Hanson hurried to the pier. Kate and the boys followed. Together they cleaned up the mess in the cabin.

Soon the weather improved enough to send a pigeon with a message. Kate wrote a note, rolled it up, and tucked it inside a tube. "We're all right, and we'll be home when it's safe to come," she told Mrs. Barclay and Grandpa.

When Anders released the pigeon, it fluttered up and winged its way off into the distance. Soon it disappeared.

By midafternoon the skies cleared off. Once more, the *Sea Gull* sailed for Duluth. On the way there, Kate, Anders, and Erik talked about what to do next. When they tied up near Booth Fisheries, they thanked Captain Hanson, then promised, "We'll let you know what happens."

As they walked toward the Corps of Engineers building, all their plans changed. A boy held up a newspaper, and Kate saw the headlines:

RANSOM NOTE SENT FOR SWEDISH WOMAN

Beneath that, in smaller letters:

WELL-KNOWN LOCAL CITIZEN RECEIVES THREATENING NOTE

Kate stared at the words, then reached for a paper. She poked Anders. "Will you pay him?"

As Anders and Erik looked over her shoulder, Kate read aloud:

A well-known local family received a ransom note about 10:00 P.M. last evening. Strangely enough, the person the note describes as being kidnapped is not missing. The woman supposedly held for ransom is safely at home with her son's family.

Businessman Nels Sundberg revealed the contents of the note to police. "We are holding your mother for ransom," it said. "If you pay the amount of money we ask, we will return her to you."

Instructions followed, telling the family where the money should be left. The last line of the note read: "If you value your mother's life, do not talk to the police."

The article ended with a telephone number and a request:

Please call if you have any information that would shed light on this mystery.

As Kate finished reading, she swallowed hard. Without warning, tears flooded her eyes, then streamed down her cheeks.

Erik caught Kate's hand and gave it a comforting squeeze. But she couldn't stop crying.

"Grandma's in real danger now," Kate said when she could speak.

Erik nodded. "Whoever that man is, he knows Grandma isn't Mr. Sundberg's mother."

"He has no more reason to take care of Grandma." Kate started crying again.

"We need to talk to Mr. Sundberg right away," Erik answered.

When they found a telephone, none of them knew how to use it. In Grantsburg, farmers had formed a telephone company, but the line was still a long way from Windy Hill Farm.

Finally Kate figured out that she needed to take the receiver off the hook and put it to her ear.

"Number, please?" a voice asked.

When Kate didn't answer quickly enough, the voice spoke again. "Number, please? Please speak into the mouthpiece."

Kate leaned forward into what she thought was the mouthpiece. She read the number from the newspaper. Soon she heard a hello from the other end of the line.

"Nels Sundberg residence."

When at last Kate turned away from the telephone, she knew what to do. "The man who answered said that Mr. Sundberg wants to talk with us. He gave directions to their house in east

Duluth. There's a train going out that way."

"Good thing we have money from turning in Grandpa's tickets," Anders said.

———

Soon after getting off the train, Kate and Anders and Erik found the Sundberg house. Flower beds lined either side of the circle drive. Tulips waved gently in the warm breeze. Still carrying the basket with the two remaining pigeons, Kate and the boys started through the well-kept yard.

Kate sniffed. What was that sweet scent? She looked up to an apple tree with branches above her head. At home the trees had bloomed earlier in May. It seemed like spring again.

The blossoms reminded her of Windy Hill Farm—of the large kitchen with everyone around the table. Kate wished she could be there with Grandma and Grandpa sitting next to her.

Now as Kate and the boys drew close to the house, large stone lions guarded either side of the door.

Anders whistled. "Too bad Lutfisk can't see those!"

For the first time since reading the newspaper, Kate smiled. If her brother's dog had been here, he would have growled. "He'd think he was protecting us!"

A woman wearing a white apron opened the door. When Anders explained who they were, she answered, "Mr. Sundberg said I should expect you."

The maid directed them into a small room at one side of the entry. "I'll tell Mr. Sundberg that you're here."

Erik sat down on a stiff-looking chair. As though afraid the spindly legs would break beneath his weight, Anders lowered himself carefully onto another chair. Kate sat on a horsehair davenport that made the back of her legs itch.

While they waited, Kate looked around the room. An oil painting hung above a richly carved table. Through an open window Kate saw an apple tree smaller than the one near the street.

Just then a man dressed in a black suit entered the room. A gold chain crossed his vest, ending at the watch pocket.

Anders and Erik jumped to their feet. Kate decided she had better stand too.

The man stretched out his hand. "I'm Nels Sundberg."

"My stepsister, Katherine O'Connell." Anders spoke with such a courteous manner that Kate felt amazed. "My friend, Erik Lundgren. I am Anders Nordstrom. We're from Trade Lake, near Grantsburg, Wisconsin."

Mr. Sundberg nodded. "Please sit down." He took the seat which Kate gladly gave up. She found a chair that didn't itch.

"I understand that your grandmother is missing."

As quickly as possible, Anders told the story.

Mr. Sundberg turned to Kate. "You saw your grandmother?" he asked. "Can you describe her for me?"

"She's tall for a woman. Her white hair waves back on both sides of her head." Kate held out the wooden carving.

Mr. Sundberg took the carving in his hands. "A very fine piece of work," he said as he studied it.

"Grandpa finished carving it after Grandma was stolen away. When we saw her, she didn't have the shawl over her head. She was wearing a fur coat."

"A fur coat?"

Kate caught the surprise in Mr. Sundberg's voice.

When Anders explained how Grandpa saved a boy's life, the man nodded again. "I see," he said.

"Grandpa thinks it's the coat that gave the problem," Kate explained. "Maybe he's right."

Mr. Sundberg stood up. "Just a minute." He pressed a button by the side of the painting.

From far away Kate heard a bell ring. Soon the maid appeared in the doorway.

"Please ask my parents to come here," Mr. Sundberg said.

Soon a man and woman appeared in the doorway. While Grandma was tall with white hair, this woman was short with light brown hair. Behind Mr. Sundberg's mother and father stood the detective who was guarding them.

"I don't understand," Kate said to Mr. Sundberg as all of them sat down again. "How could someone think Grandma was your mother?"

The businessman shook his head as though wondering himself. "All I know is that my parents came into Union Depot a day late."

"That explains it!" Kate said. "The man who was lurking around outside the depot! He heard that your parents were supposed to come from Sweden. Then he saw Grandma and Grandpa that afternoon. Grandma looked like she was rich. The man probably thought he could get ransom money from you."

"But there's something more," Erik said quietly. "From what we've heard, the man may be holding a grudge against you."

Mr. Sundberg nodded. "That makes sense. If that man and the one in the checked suit are the same person, he could be trying to get even."

Mr. Sundberg thought for a moment. "Not long ago I had to let someone go because he never did his work. He always made trouble with everyone. His name was Jonas."

Kate looked at Erik. Both of them looked at Anders. They were back to the same thing. They needed to find Jonas.

As they stood up to leave, Mr. Sundberg said he would telephone the police and tell them what he knew. "Where are you staying?" he asked.

Anders gave him the address, and Mr. Sundberg promised, "I'll contact you there if we find out anything. Now I'll see that you get a ride home."

Instead of ringing for the maid again, he led them outside to the carriage house. Through an open door, Anders spotted an automobile.

"A Pierce-Arrow," he whispered to Erik. Both boys craned their necks, trying to see.

Mr. Sundberg led them toward a large carriage. He tipped his head toward the driver. "He'll see that you get to Mrs. Barclay's safely."

Erik and Anders shook Mr. Sundberg's hand.

"Thank you," Kate said as she, too, climbed into the carriage. "It's kind of you to help us."

Mr. Sundberg shook his head. "Not kind at all. My own mother isn't safe until that man is caught."

19

Another Threat!

$\mathcal{T}$he driver flicked the reins, and the pair of high-stepping black horses pranced down the driveway. Never had Kate ridden in such a carriage. But she felt too troubled to lean back and rest against the cushions.

"We're out of time, aren't we?" she asked. "If Jonas has seen that newspaper, he knows he has the wrong person."

"From what his sister told us, he has to be somewhere in Duluth," Erik answered.

"But where?" Kate asked. "There are so many places to hide. We have to narrow it down."

Suddenly Anders had an idea. "The footsteps! Remember? The night of the fog we heard them right after we left the canal."

Both Erik and Kate nodded.

"We were just starting to go through the area with all the boardinghouses. And guess what was behind us!"

"The canal," Kate said.

"And Minnesota Point! I bet Jonas is hiding out on Minnesota Point!"

"You might be right," Kate said slowly. She turned it over in her mind. "Yes, I think you *are!*"

Erik grinned. "I think so too! I bet that's where Jonas's wife stayed. When he went up the North Shore, I mean. So let's look on the peninsula!"

Anders leaned toward the driver. "Will you take us to the canal instead?"

As the driver changed directions, Anders decided to release the second pigeon. "I'll tell Mrs. Barclay where we're going. She can tell the police."

While Kate held the pigeon, Anders fastened the message tube to its leg. When the pigeon flew up, it headed straight toward the hill above the business district.

When they reached the canal, the driver stopped the carriage close to the aerial bridge. The transfer car was loading passengers. With Anders carrying the last remaining pigeon, the three hurried on. Soon the gates closed and the car moved out across the canal.

The ride to Minnesota Point took a little over a minute. From inside the cabin, Kate stared down at the dark water. As the car drew near to the south pier, she noticed what looked like a square manhole cover.

"That's it!" she exclaimed to Anders.

"What's *it*, my dear sister?"

"See?" Kate pointed. "Remember what Captain Hanson said? That must be the entrance to the tunnel."

She looked down the long pier. Sure enough, the manhole lined up with the lighthouse.

When the transfer car landed, Kate and the boys set off on the road down the center of the peninsula. As they followed the trolley tracks, they studied every building they passed.

After several blocks, the sun slipped below the horizon. Anders stopped right in the middle of the street. "How long is this peninsula, anyway?"

Erik grinned. "I've heard it's a five or six mile walk."

Anders groaned. "Maybe I didn't have such a good idea, after all."

But Kate had noticed a tumbledown house that seemed deserted. "There!" she exclaimed. "Doesn't that look like a good hideout?"

She started toward the house, but then a bell clanged. Whirling around, Kate looked back in the direction from which they had walked. With its headlight on, a trolley was coming down the track.

As the bell continued to clang, doors flew open on both sides of the road. People ran out of their houses. Men raced for the trolley and jumped on. Standing on a narrow footboard, they clung to the side of the trolley.

"Well, don't just stand there!" said a woman next to Anders. "Don't you know you're supposed to help?"

Already the men were pulling on long rubber coats and firemen's helmets. Anders and Erik ran for the car. As they jumped onto a step, Kate saw ladders and hoses on the side of the trolley.

"It's a fire car?" she asked.

"Well, certainly," the woman answered. "Only one like it in the whole United States! Offers us good protection!" she added proudly.

Kate stared down the track. Several blocks away, smoke rose above one of the buildings. She started walking in that direction, then glanced back toward the small frame house she had noticed. Earlier, the house had looked empty. Now two faces gazed from the window.

One of the women had brown hair, drawn straight back in a bun. Somehow the face seemed familiar.

Then Kate noticed the second woman. *It has to be Grandma!*

In the next instant the brown-haired woman looked toward Kate. The two faces disappeared from the window.

———

In the fading light Kate stood there, staring. Finally she remembered. *If it's really Grandma, I can't give myself away.*

Turning, she walked quickly in the direction of the fire. After passing several buildings, she crossed the street, then slipped behind the nearest house.

The backyard opened onto sand dunes. Kate climbed the

dune and dropped down on the other side. The deep blue waters of Lake Superior lay in front of her. To her left was the house she had noticed.

Kate set off in that direction. When she believed she was far enough, she climbed the dune. Standing at the top, she looked down. The house was in even worse condition than she thought.

A large tree lay between Kate and the building. Another tree on the side of the house offered good protection from anyone who might look from the street.

Kate glanced around. On either side, the yards were empty. *Should I risk it?*

Soon the twilight would change to darkness. By then Anders and Erik would be looking for her. And what about Grandma? *How long can I wait?*

Kate ran for the nearest tree. The back door stood open, swinging in the breeze from the lake. A murmur of voices reached her.

Kate strained to hear. Close to the farthest tree, a window was open.

Staying low, Kate crept forward. When she knelt down beneath the window, she could hear every word.

Soft and low, a woman spoke Swedish. Kate had heard the same voice at Central High School. It was Grandma, all right!

A second woman answered in English. "Are you hungry?"

"No." Kate understood the Swedish.

"Is there anything you need?" The voice sounded harsh, yet at the same time willing to help.

When there was no answer, the woman repeated the question. Another silence followed, and Kate felt sure her grandmother didn't understand.

How awful to be a stranger in a strange country, Kate thought. *Not to understand, even when someone offers help!*

"Do what we say, and my husband won't hurt you," the woman warned.

In that moment Kate changed her mind. She felt glad that Grandma might not understand.

"My husband left to talk with someone," the woman went

on. "When he comes back, we'll go away."

Kate stood up and found herself looking into a kitchen. The brown-haired woman sat with her back to the window. Across the table and facing the window sat the woman Kate believed to be Grandma. As she glanced toward Kate, her eyes widened. Yet she looked away and spoke in Swedish. She sounded calm, as if nothing had happened.

Ducking down again, Kate crept forward along the side of the house. When she reached the front, she peered around the tree.

Anders and Erik were coming down the street. In the growing darkness, Kate ran to meet them.

"We got there so fast, the fire's out!" Anders told her.

But Kate whispered, "I found Grandma!"

She led them off the road to a safe distance away from the small house. "There's a woman with her. It must be Jonas's wife, Stella. She said her husband would come soon, and they would go away."

"Then we don't have much time," Erik said. "What can we do?"

"Grandma knows who I am." Believing that made Kate feel good inside. "Whatever we plan, Grandma needs to see me. Then she'll know it's safe to go with us."

"Why don't we use *their* trick?" Anders asked. "Jonas fooled Grandma into thinking something was wrong with Grandpa. I'll get Stella away from the house."

"If you lead her to the end of the peninsula, Kate and I can take Grandma the opposite way—across the canal," Erik said.

"I'll do the talking!" Anders said as they started back to the house.

"How can you do it without lying?" Kate asked.

"Just leave everything to me." Her brother's eyes shone with laughter. "We'll get Grandma away. You betcha!"

But Kate felt uneasy. *If only nothing goes wrong!*

While Anders knocked, Erik and Kate hid around the corner of the house. After a brief wait, they heard the door creak open.

"Are you Jonas's wife, Stella?" Anders asked.

"Why, yes, I am." Kate heard the fear in the woman's voice. "Did something happen to him?"

"I'm sorry to have to ask this," Anders said, his voice as solemn as Kate had ever heard it. "I need to have you come with me."

The door creaked again. "Is there something wrong with my husband?"

"I'll take you where you need to go."

"Oh! I've always been afraid that something like this would happen!" Stella turned back and called to Grandma. "You stay right here!"

Anders started toward the street. "Hurry," he said. "It's important that you come at once."

"Where is Jonas?" Stella asked as she followed Anders.

"Don't waste time talking." Anders walked quickly now. "Just come with me."

As soon as Stella's back was turned, Kate and Erik slipped into the house.

"Grandma?" Kate called softly, not wanting to frighten her. In the light of a kerosene lantern she saw the white-haired woman.

"Grandma?" Kate asked again, suddenly shy before this person she had never met. "Are you my grandmother?"

With an ease surprising for her age, the woman stood up. "You are Kate?" she asked in Swedish. As she opened her arms, Kate hurried across the room.

"My Kate! My Kate!" Grandma murmured over and over. "My granddaughter!"

Kate's throat tightened. In spite of all she wanted to say, she could not speak.

But Erik did. "Kate, we have to hurry." He spoke quickly in Swedish, explaining to Grandma.

"Go!" she answered in English. She caught up a cloth bag with wooden handles and hurried to the door.

Anders and the woman were out of sight. Erik led Grandma and Kate in the opposite direction.

Once Erik stopped and spoke to Grandma in Swedish. When

Grandma answered, Erik explained to Kate. "She's used to hard work on the farm," he said. "It's all right to walk fast."

A block from the house, Kate remembered the last pigeon. "Oh, Erik, where is it? We might need it."

"When we ran for the fire car, Anders set it down."

Kate hurried back. To her relief the basket still sat along the side of the road.

As Kate returned to Grandma and Erik, a trolley caught up with them. Grandma dug into her bag. When she opened her hand, the palm was filled with coins. Erik picked out three nickels, and they climbed aboard.

Next to the aerial bridge they left the trolley. The transfer car was loading passengers on the city side of the canal. As Kate watched, she grew more and more uneasy.

"I don't like it," she whispered to Erik. "Jonas could come at any time, and we're out in the open."

Kate looked up at Grandma. Here, close to the inner range light, her hair seemed even whiter and more noticeable. If only there was a way to cover it! But Grandma had left her shawl behind.

Again Kate turned to Erik. "Do you remember when you talked about feeling uneasy?"

Erik nodded.

"I've never been so uneasy in my life. Do you think God is warning me?"

"It's more than being scared?"

Kate nodded. "I think so."

"I'm uneasy too. Something's wrong. I'll get the last pigeon ready, just in case."

Erik set down the basket, wrote a note asking for help from the police, and slipped it inside a tube. Kate attached the message holder to the pigeon's leg.

When Erik stood up again, Grandma was watching. Erik explained in Swedish, and Grandma nodded.

A moment later, the transfer car finished taking on passengers and started toward them. Suddenly a thought popped into

Kate's head. *If I had to hide, where could I go?* The idea startled her.

She looked around, searching. Near at hand, the range light shone down on the south pier. If she and Grandma stood on the other side of the light, would it hide them?

As Kate looked back to the transfer car, she saw a man next to the railing. Kate stared at him. Tall with a mustache. A bowler hat and checked suit.

Then Grandma grabbed Kate's arm and pointed. In that same moment the man looked their way.

"It's Jonas!" Erik whispered.

Kate's stomach churned. *Did he see Grandma?* She felt sure he did.

"I'll take Grandma behind the range light," Kate said.

"I'll try to draw his attention to the pigeon," Erik answered. "When you think it's safe, get Grandma on the bridge."

Erik moved away and Kate tucked her hand inside her grandmother's elbow. "Stay with me," she whispered, and hoped that Grandma understood.

Quickly Kate led her to the range light and slipped around on the other side. The tall thin tower offered little protection. Steel girders kept them from standing as close to the tower as needed.

It's not enough, Kate thought, the panic within her growing. *What can I do?*

Then she remembered the manhole for the tunnel under the pier. Kate tugged on Grandma's arm and started to run. Grandma followed, walking fast.

When they reached the opening, Kate lifted the cover and pointed. The range light shone into the hole, lighting a floor three feet below.

Holding Kate's hand, Grandma stepped down on a steel rung, then onto the floor. Kate jumped in beside her. Crouching low, she dropped the cover. A darkness deeper than night surrounded them.

20

Hide-and-Seek Darkness

*T*he darkness closed in around Kate. Without even a pinprick of light, she felt as if her head were spinning.

"Kate?" Grandma asked softly. "You are here?"

Kate understood the simple Swedish words. "Yes, I am here," she said, glad for the sound of her grandmother's voice.

"The man. He will come?"

Again Kate understood. "He might come," she answered. "He saw us, I think."

"What?" Clearly Grandma could not follow her explanation.

"He might come," Kate repeated.

"He is a bad man," answered Grandma.

Kate shifted her position. As she tried to move, she bumped her head against the low ceiling. On hands and knees, she reached out, feeling her way around the darkness.

The tunnel seemed about six feet wide. The ceiling rounded in an arch only three feet above the floor.

Soon Kate discovered a long, narrow board with wheels on the underside. A dolly. Or should she call it a carriage? *Maybe the keeper used it for carrying things out to the lighthouse*, Kate thought.

The small wheels of the carriage rode on a track extending into the darkness. What would they find if they went that direction? *If only I had a candle! Just one small candle!*

Kate reached out, trying to judge the size of the carriage. Instead, her hands touched something wet and cold.

She jerked back, trying to get away. Again Kate bumped her head. Then she realized what she had felt.

Water.

Kate's heart thudded. "The tunnel floods with high seas," the captain had said. How much came in during the storm? Had it drained out? Kate had no way of knowing.

Telling herself to be calm, she wiped her hands on her skirt. *A grown man goes through this tunnel?* Kate wondered how he could do it. *He must have to lie down on the carriage.*

Reaching up, she rubbed her bruised head. *Betsy's hair ribbon! When did I lose it?*

Again Kate wished for a candle, for even one crack of light. The darkness seemed alive.

Instead, she heard a noise above her—the thud of heavy boots on a steel door. She reached out, found Grandma's hand. Together they crept back, away from the trapdoor.

A moment later it lifted. Light slanted into the hole. In silence Kate and Grandma waited.

"Hello?" came a man's voice. Was it Jonas?

"Hello, down there!" It was Jonas, all right.

Kate reached up, put her hand over Grandma's lips. But Grandma understood. Fumbling in the dark, she placed her own hand across Kate's mouth.

"Hello?" the voice asked again.

Kate pressed back, away from the light coming through the manhole. As she leaned into the wall, something brushed across her face. A scream rose in her throat.

Just in time Kate held it back. *A spider web,* she told herself.

But the terror within her grew. Her hands clenched as she thought of a spider crawling across her face.

After a long silence, the trapdoor slammed down. Once again, darkness filled the tunnel.

"Jonas come back?" Grandma whispered.

"Maybe he went for a candle," Kate answered. The man had waited as though he knew where they were. Why? What had given them away?

An awful thought struck Kate. *That must be where I lost Betsy's bow—just beneath the trapdoor!*

It was too late to go back and find it. The damage had already been done. Kate forgot her fear of water and spiders. She had only one thought—escaping from Jonas.

Kate tugged at Grandma's arm. "Come," she said.

When she felt the carriage again, Kate took Grandma's hand and helped her touch it. The long narrow board was only a short distance above the track.

"Lie down," Kate said.

When Grandma didn't understand, Kate lay down with her back on the board. As soon as she crawled off again, Grandma took Kate's place.

On her knees, Kate grasped hold of the end of the carriage and pushed. To her surprise it moved easily.

Turning around, Kate dropped down on the end of the carriage, next to Grandma's shoes. With hunched shoulders and head low, Kate sat with her face almost in her lap. Then she pushed with her feet. The carriage moved off down the track.

How far? Kate wondered. She struggled to remember the pier as she'd seen it from outside. A quarter of a mile perhaps? In her memory the pier stretched away forever.

They had gone only a short distance when water seeped through Kate's shoes. She stopped pushing and slipped her hand down along the side of the carriage. The water was getting deeper.

Suddenly Kate felt closed in by concrete. It wouldn't take much flooding to fill the tunnel. *What if we're trapped by water, unable to breathe?*

Kate froze with the terror of it. *What should I do?*

If you need wisdom . . . As though someone had spoken, she remembered the words. *Ask for it.*

"Jesus—" Kate prayed, so afraid that she could say no more. Her throat tightened as the word echoed, bouncing off the walls of the tunnel.

To go back seemed unthinkable. Jonas could come at any time. But what if they reached the end of the tunnel and there was no way out?

For an instant Kate waited. *Believe, without doubting.*

Again she pushed off. Several feet farther on, she reached down. Three, perhaps four inches of water covered the floor, but now Kate had hope. *If it doesn't get any deeper, we're safe.*

Her soaked feet set up a rhythm. Left, right, left, right.

"Kate?" Grandma asked.

"Yes, Grandma?"

"You all right?"

"I'm all right." Kate reached back to squeeze Grandma's hand and lost her balance. Her feet broke the rhythm. In the stillness Kate heard a steel door slam.

Kate gasped. Someone had entered the tunnel! Though her feet felt like lead weights, she gave a mighty push.

Far off, she saw the glow of a candle and a man's hand holding it. Jonas!

For the first time, Kate felt glad that she had no candle. With all her strength she pushed the carriage, trying hard to make no sound.

Was Jonas coming through the tunnel? Crawling on hands and knees? Kate couldn't be sure, but the candle seemed to move closer. As though living a nightmare, Kate kept on.

How far? she wondered again. *How far to the lighthouse?*

Her legs ached now. She wanted to cry out, to scream, *I can't do it!* But the candle moved steadily closer.

Then the carriage bumped to a stop. Kate fell onto the floor. Water soaked through her skirt.

Pulling herself to her knees, Kate leaned toward her grandmother. "Wait," she whispered, and hoped that Grandma understood.

Reaching out, Kate discovered a rock wall. As she felt along the wall, something ran over her hand.

Kate clamped a hand over her mouth, held back a scream. *What was it? How many more?*

Still shaking, she tried to stand up. Her head no longer bumped the ceiling. This time Kate's hand felt a steel rung. Then another. A ladder!

As she turned to her grandmother, Kate stared down the long dark tunnel. The light had moved closer.

Kate found her grandmother's hand and tugged. When the older woman stood up, Kate whispered in her ear. "Ladder."

Grandma remained still as if unsure what to do. Kate pulled her toward the rock wall, then guided Grandma's hand to the iron rung.

Again Kate looked back. The man was gaining on them.

"Me first," she whispered. "You come."

Kate grabbed one rung, then another. As quickly as possible, she climbed the ladder.

Then Kate's head bumped against something. Still clinging to a rung, she reached up. Her free hand felt a steel trapdoor.

Kate pushed against it. The door refused to budge.

21

Grandpa's Gifts

*U*sing her free hand, Kate pushed again. Still the heavy door would not open. With only one hand, she did not have enough strength.

The fear within her growing, she looked down. A trace of light filtered through the opening around the ladder. Jonas was almost here!

Desperate with panic, Kate reached out, found another rung. When she stepped up, her back pressed into the trapdoor. It moved.

Kate climbed farther, and the door swung open against a wall. Kate stepped out into a large room.

Grandma was right behind her. Kate helped her through the square hole, then dropped the door. The clang of steel echoed through the building.

Kate jumped onto the trapdoor. "We made it!"

A minute later, Kate felt the door move beneath her. As the steel trembled, she cried out. "Stand on it!"

Grandma stared at her, but did not move. Kate pointed down. "Stand!"

As her grandmother stepped onto the door, it settled back in place.

"Help!" Kate called. "Help!"

A man appeared through a doorway on the far side of the room. "Help?" he asked. "Where did you come from?"

"Through the tunnel. A man followed us." Kate's words spilled out so fast that the lightkeeper asked her to stop.

"I don't understand. Where is the man now?"

"Under my feet," Kate answered. "Please," she pleaded. "Help me put something heavy on the door."

The lightkeeper swung around, searching for what he could use. Grabbing up a shovel, he filled three big buckets with coal. He set the heavy buckets on the trapdoor.

In the light of the room Kate had her first long look at her grandmother. In spite of all she had gone through, Grandma stood straight and tall. But her hands trembled.

"Is there a chair?" Kate asked.

The lightkeeper bounded across the room and up a narrow stairway. Through a window, Kate saw him hurry into a room overlooking the area where she stood. When the lightkeeper returned, he carried a chair.

Grandma sank onto it. "You all right, Kate?" she asked.

"I'm all right," Kate answered softly. Even in this moment, Grandma's first thought was about her.

Kate pointed at Grandma. "And you?"

"Yah, I am good." Grandma's smile lit her eyes. But her beautiful hair fell around her face. Streaks of dirt darkened her cheeks.

"You stay here. You're safe." Kate motioned with her hands. "You rest."

Grandma nodded, and Kate turned to the lightkeeper. "We need to tell someone to catch the man as he comes out of the tunnel."

The lightkeeper hurried through a door to the tower. He led Kate up a spiral staircase.

As she stepped out at the top, she felt the heat of the light. Then she saw the prisms—dozens of pieces of glass surrounding the light. Its powerful beam reached out across Lake Superior and back toward the aerial bridge.

Kate turned in that direction. The transfer car was moving across the canal toward Minnesota Point. Anders stood along the south pier. Next to him was Jonas's wife. To Kate's surprise Stella waited quietly, almost as if she were relieved to be caught.

A moment later the transfer car landed. Erik and four policemen stepped off. As they reached Anders, one of the men took charge of Stella.

"Erik!" Kate called, then realized he couldn't hear through the glass of the lighthouse. She turned to the lightkeeper.

"That's Erik, my friend!" Kate pointed down. "We have to tell the policemen!"

The lightkeeper opened a door. As he moved onto the narrow walkway outside the tower, Kate followed. Once she looked down, saw the distance to the pier, and stopped. Then, clinging to the railing, she moved on.

When she reached the side toward the aerial bridge, Kate shouted, "Erik!" When he didn't turn, Kate cupped her hands around her mouth and called again.

"Erik!" the lightkeeper shouted.

Erik swung around, looked toward the light. Kate waved.

Erik called to the policemen, pointed toward the lighthouse. The three men started running.

"Stop!" Kate called.

"Stop!" the lightkeeper repeated.

Kate pointed toward the trapdoor near the range light. At first Erik didn't understand. Then he saw the entrance to the tunnel. Pointing at it, he looked toward Kate. She nodded.

Sergeant Holmquist and two other policemen gathered around the trapdoor. While Kate watched, the door lifted, then swung back. When Jonas climbed out, the policemen closed in around him.

As Anders and Eric started toward the lighthouse, Kate edged her way around the walkway into the tower. Once there, she scrambled down the spiral staircase. At the bottom of the steps she hurried through the large room, then found a door opening onto the pier.

As Anders ran up, he stared at Kate. "You are a sight!"

Kate remembered the dirt on Grandma's cheeks and wiped her own. But as Kate pushed back her hair, she saw her brother's face. For the second time that week Kate knew that he really cared about what happened to her.

Then Erik reached Kate. "You look *wonderful!*" he said.

Kate sneaked a look at Anders. He was staring at his friend.

"Are you all right?" Erik asked Kate. "I got on the bridge and couldn't find you." His eyes still showed his fear. "Where did you go?"

Kate started to explain, then remembered. "Anders hasn't met my grandmother."

As she spoke the words, her heart leaped. *My grandmother. Grandpa's stolen treasure. And my treasure too!*

Kate led the way back into the lighthouse. With a warm smile Grandma stood up and held out her hands to the boys. Watching her, Kate felt proud.

Anders said something to Grandma in Swedish. She nodded, then turned to Kate. Reaching out, she circled Kate with her arm.

"This is my granddaughter," Grandma said. The words sounded stiff, as though Grandma had worked hard to learn the English.

Quick tears filled Kate's eyes. Her grandmother's arms tightened around her. "I am proud of Kate."

They thanked the lightkeeper, then set out, back along the south pier toward the aerial bridge. When they reached the policemen, Sergeant Holmquist told them that the homing pigeons had carried their messages without a problem.

He spoke in Swedish to Grandma. "This is the man?"

Grandma nodded her head. "This is the wicked man who stole me away."

As Erik translated for Kate, Grandma turned to Stella and spoke again. "This is his wife, but she is not wicked. She took good care of me, even though she was afraid of her husband."

———

When Grandpa saw Grandma, he opened his arms, then

closed them around his treasure. Tears streamed down his cheeks.

As soon as the police had all the information they needed, Mrs. Barclay took them to Union Depot and sent a telegram to Mama.

"I will see you onto the train!" Mrs. Barclay exclaimed. "I will take no chances about you getting where you are supposed to go."

Just before the train left, Mrs. Barclay gave Anders two large baskets with young pigeons for starting his own loft.

Then Grandma opened her bag with the wooden handles. Taking out something wrapped in a cloth, she handed it to Mrs. Barclay. When the cloth fell away, Kate saw a small fishing boat.

"I carved it on the trip across the ocean," Grandpa said. "Maybe Captain Hanson would like it. You will give it to him?"

"I will give it to him," Mrs. Barclay answered, her voice solemn. Then her eyes sparkled with laughter. "I will invite him for supper to be sure that he gets it."

Once more, Grandma reached into her bag. Once more, Mrs. Barclay opened a piece of cloth. This time she held up a carving of a woman holding a tray filled with food.

"It is you," Grandpa said, his voice gruff. "We thank you."

"And I thank *you*," answered Mrs. Barclay. "I will always remember you and your family."

On the way to Rush City, Grandpa sat next to Grandma. Every now and then his hand reached out and covered hers. He looked as though he would never again let Grandma out of his sight.

Anders sat next to Kate in a seat facing her grandparents. Partway home, she remembered that this train went on to Minneapolis. *I wonder if I'll ever go back for a visit? If I'll ever see Sarah Livingston again? And Michael Reilly? What is he like by now?*

As the train rushed past trees and farms, Kate thought about it. Often her friends had teased Michael, saying, "You're sweet on Kate." Michael never denied it.

I wonder if he's as nice as Erik. Kate glanced across the aisle and found Erik looking at her.

When they changed trains at Rush City, his voice was filled with excitement. "Did you notice the person sitting next to me? He's an advance man for a circus."

"A *circus*?" Kate asked. "Wouldn't it be fun to go to one?"

"The man is traveling ahead, making plans to bring his circus into the area. Maybe it'll be close enough to go."

Soon after they climbed aboard the train to Grantsburg, Grandma reached into her bag again. This time she pulled out the carving Kate had carried all around Duluth.

"It is yours," Grandma said, as she put it into Kate's hands.

Kate looked down to the carving of her grandmother. With a shawl around her head, the woman sat on a three-legged stool. In her hands she held what seemed to be knitting needles.

Again Kate touched the tiny face, the hollows in her grandmother's cheeks. For the rest of her life Kate would remember the meaning of this gift.

"When we get to the farm, I'll paint it for you," Grandpa promised.

Kate looked up. An even greater treasure—her grandparents—sat right in front of her!

The rest of the way home, Grandpa and Grandma talked, telling them about Sweden. Erik and Anders translated for Kate.

Grandpa looked at Anders, then at Erik. "Both of you are good grandsons!" he said.

Erik glanced quickly at Kate and winked. But Kate guessed what Grandpa's words meant to him.

The two grandparents also had questions. "Ben will be there?" Grandpa asked more than once. Each time Kate or the boys said yes, he turned to Grandma. "We came all this way to find Ben, and he is found!"

When the train pulled into Grantsburg, Kate was the first to get off. Papa stood on the platform, holding baby Bernie. Next to him were Lars, and Tina, and Mama. But where was Ben?

Then Kate walked into Mama's arms. Tina clung to both of them. Lars stood off to one side, as if embarrassed by all this emotion in public.

Again Kate looked around. If Ben wasn't here, Grandpa and

Grandma would be sick with disappointment.

With her hand inside Erik's arm, Grandma stepped down from the train. She moved quickly as if years younger than she was.

Anders helped Grandpa. His knee was still stiff, but his eyes searched for his family.

Then he and Grandma stood before Mama. Mama flung one arm around Grandma, the other arm around Grandpa.

"I can't believe it!" Mama exclaimed when she finally stood back. "You're really here!"

She turned to introduce Papa, Lars, Tina, and the new baby. Even Lutfisk was there, wagging his tail.

"And Ben?" Grandma asked, as if worried that even now she could be disappointed.

Then Kate saw him, standing at one side of the depot, as though afraid to join the family. Kate ran to Ben and pulled him forward.

As the tall nineteen-year-old walked slowly toward his parents, Grandpa stood straighter.

"Ah, Ben," he said. "All this long way we have come to see you."

"To see *me*?" Ben asked, still unbelieving.

"To see *you*," Grandma answered. "Your sister Ingrid is important. Kate is important. But we came to see *you*."

"But why?" Ben looked as if he didn't believe their words. "I stole from a shopkeeper. I disgraced our good family name."

"And you asked forgiveness," Grandma said. "You asked the shopkeeper's forgiveness."

"We came to tell you that you are forgiven," Grandpa said. "By the shopkeeper, yah."

Grandpa stood back, looked up into the face of his tall son. "And you are forgiven by us."

As though unsure that he had really heard the words, Ben closed his eyes. When he opened them again, he gazed first at Grandpa, then at Grandma. Suddenly he bent down and wrapped his long arms around their shoulders.

Kate swallowed hard. *You're home now, Ben,* she thought. *All of us are home.*

Acknowledgments

For many years my family and I have enjoyed vacation get-aways in the Twin Ports of Duluth, Minnesota, and Superior, Wisconsin. Yet when I gathered information for this novel, I discovered a new side to all that I was seeing.

I found it fun to dig deeper—to find out more than I knew as a tourist. If you, too, are as curious as Kate, you'll still be able to see many of the sites that she and Anders and Erik visited.

At the former Union Depot, now called The Depot, you'll find the St. Louis County Heritage and Arts Center. There you can see Depot Square and discover the look and feel of Duluth in 1910, about the time that Kate visited the city. You can climb aboard old-time locomotives or a trolley restored by the Lake Superior Museum of Transportation.

You can also visit the A. M. Chisholm Museum and the Immigrant Room where Kate and the boys first saw Grandpa. On the main floor, you'll walk through the Depot's Great Hall, the waiting room that once was a busy center for people traveling in and out of Duluth. Nearby, in the Performing Arts Wing, you'll find the two masks Kate noticed on either side of the Lyceum entrance.

The tunnel inside the pier and the Spalding Hotel are gone, but you can locate both of them as well as the site of the Incline

Railway. The old Central High School is now used as an administration building for the Duluth Public Schools.

The aerial bridge has also changed—from a transfer car to a roadway that lifts up and down. Near that famous crossing you'll see the U.S. Army Corps of Engineers Building and the Canal Park Museum. You can stand as Kate, Anders, and Erik did—along the pier watching the great ships sail through the canal.

Across the bay in Superior, Wisconsin, the Fraser Shipyards now occupy the site once used by Alexander McDougall and his American Steel Barge Company. On nearby Barker's Island you'll find the S.S. *Meteor,* the last remaining whaleback ship.

Wherever I went in researching this novel, I found people friendly and helpful. Always they worked to give me the information I needed. With each interview I came away feeling as if I had gained a new friend.

My warm thanks to Patricia Maus, administrator of the St. Louis County Historical Society's Northeast Minnesota Historical Center, for the great variety of ways in which she helped me.

In addition to providing information, three people read portions of the manuscript and offered excellent suggestions: Pat Castellano, Director of Programs, A. M. Chisholm Museum; Hazel Hanson, retired teacher for the Duluth Public Schools; and C. Patrick Labadie, U.S. Army Corps of Engineers' Canal Park Museum.

Captain Stanley Sivertson and his wife Clara of Sivertson Fisheries gave valuable insights into the North Shore fishing industry. Irish storyteller Captain Gerry Downes of Cat's Paw Charters explained the ways of Lake Superior.

Thanks, too, to Mike Armstrong, Chief Engineer, Central Administration Building, Duluth Public Schools; Stephen Chandler, Petty Officer, U.S. Coast Guard; Leo McDonnell, Director, Lake Superior Museum of Transportation; Bertha Pederson and Toinie Rajala of the Chris Jensen Nursing Home; and Dan Woods, tour guide, S.S. *Meteor.*

I am also indebted to the *Duluth News-Tribune*, to Barbara Sommer, Project Director, North Shore Commercial Fishing Oral History Project, to Ryck Lydecker and Lawrence J. Sommer, editors of *Duluth: Sketches of the Past*, and the following authors: William D. Coventry, *Duluth's Age of Brownstone*; John Fritzen, *Historic Sites and Place Names of Minnesota's North Shore*; Thom Holden for his article, "Lake Superior's Wicked November Storms," in *Mariners Weather Log*, Fall 1991; Dr. Julius F. Wolff Jr., Lake Superior Shipwrecks; Frank A. Young, *Duluth's Ship Canal and Aerial Bridge*.

My gratitude also to Marita Karlisch, Archivist/Librarian, the American Swedish Institute, Minneapolis; Mark Esping, Institute of Central Kansas, Lindsborg; Tom Benson for his help with homing pigeons, and my father, Alvar Walfrid, for his experience with broncos.

As often happens with this series, the idea for this novel came from a little gem of truth. Berdella Johnson of Grantsburg, Wisconsin, told me about two immigrants in her husband's family. Theodore and Annie Jernstrom traveled safely from Sweden to America, yet missed the Rush City, Minnesota, stop and went on to Duluth.

Special thanks to you, Berdella, and other friends in the Grantsburg area: Alton Jensen, Walter and Ella Johnson, Arlene Erickson, and the Grantsburg Public Library.

As always, I have been helped by my faithful editors—Charette Barta, Doris Holmlund, and Ron Klug—and the Bethany team. My husband Roy has given daily encouragement and shared the good times that helped inspire this book.